I think we can all agree that the world needs more sapphic pirates!

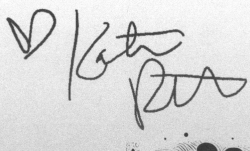

TO KIDNAP A PRINCESS

DANGEROUS TIDES

KATEE ROBERT

TRINKETS & TALES LLC

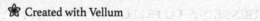

CONTENT NOTES

Tropes: Reunited lovers

Tags: FF romance, I'll always come for you, childhood friends to lovers to something more complicated to lovers, oh my god do not touch that or that or that oh shit you're going to get us killed, plus sized heroine, the pirate and the princess, if you're not going to kidnap me then I guess I'll kidnap myself, I want to RUIN you for anyone else,

Content Warnings: Explicit sex, blood, violence, murder, threat of sexual assault (non-explicit, briefly referenced), near-drowning

1

JULIETTE

Kidnapping myself was the easy part. I know the guards' schedules like the back of my hand. I grew up in the castle, dodging nannies and tutors in favor of playing in the cove where the waves kiss the rocky shore. I left my pack tucked behind one of my mother's rose-bushes, filled with enough gold sewn into the lining to make my back ache, some snacks, and a particularly inspired piece of lingerie to impress Maura with.

I made it to the docks in record time and identified the agreed-upon ship, a wicked-looking one with a mermaid carved into the bow and nine-pointed star on the sails. *The Drowning Maid*. The captain even welcomed me warmly, walking into his quarters...

Where he chained me to the desk and left.

"It seems I've made a mistake." This was only supposed to be a pretend kidnapping, a way to get me out of the castle and far enough from land to use the piece of eight I may or may not have lifted off that Cŵn Annwn ambassador. I was going to impress Maura with my cleverness so she'd see that I am finally a worthy partner.

Unfortunately, it looks like I'm going to need a rescue after all.

The ship sways a bit. My stomach flips; we must be leaving the docks. I'm not an innocent, no matter that I've lived my entire life in the castle I was born in. I know what men like these are capable of. I've read the books and listened to the reports delivered to my father. I'd like to think *these* pirates aren't the same kind of men as the ones from *those* reports, but this kidnapping has become unfortunately nonconsensual.

If we reach the open sea...

Damn it, there's no help for it. Guess I have to be Maura's damsel in distress.

With a muttered curse, I twist around to reach the ring on my chained hand. It's a lovely thing, though its bronze is slightly discolored with age. The sapphire isn't particularly large, but it's clear and pretty.

I hesitate, but there's no time to waste. Maura's ship, *The Kelpie*, was last seen half a world away. Even with magic speeding the journey, it might take her days to reach me.

If she even comes...

No, I can't think like that. Maura will come for me. She gave me this ring the last time I saw her, sixteen and filled with so much hope for the future. I can still feel the sun on my face and her strong hand gripping mine as she slid it onto my finger.

A promise, love. I might not be back for a while, not until I've made a name for myself, but I will be back for you. If you need me, I will come for you.

Even though so much has changed between us in the time since then, surely *that* hasn't. I didn't doubt that she'd still want me when I put this plan into place, and I can't doubt it now.

Before I can talk myself out of it—and I'm very good at talking myself into and out of things—I twist the gem until I feel a click. I inhale, and magic courses out in a pulse that makes my skin buzz.

No taking it back now.

I arrange my robe around me and slump back against the desk. *This is so ridiculous.*

The ship sways as we continue to cut through the water. I haven't traveled much outside of one-day excursions, and my stomach makes a sickening dip in time with the waves.

Oh gods, am I going to get seasick?

Truly, this is a mess of epic proportions.

To distract myself, I look around the cabin. It's nice enough, I suppose. I don't know what a captain's quarters normally look like. These might have started quite luxurious, but there's wear and tear visible everywhere from the pitted wooden floor beneath me to the chipped and stained desk that smells faintly of stale alcohol, to the shabby hammock that hangs in the corner. There's another smell that I want nothing to do with coming from that corner.

I...did not think this through.

The swaying of the ship picks up until it feels like we're skimming over the waves. The lurch makes my stomach twist and spiral.

I examine the chains. I could pick the lock...probably...but that's only a temporary solution.

Still, better than nothing.

The captain didn't search me before he locked me in here, so it only takes a few minutes to work the lock with the picks in my pocket. It clicks open almost silently. "Well, that's something."

I stand and shake my hand a bit, working the tingles out. I suppose the next thing to do is find a weapon. The thought makes me sigh. My father's weapons master says I'm hopeless at combat. Too distractible. Too often spouting quick quips instead of finding my opponent's weakness and exploiting it.

"Plan, plan, I need a plan." Now's not the time to get distracted.

I drag in a breath and start snooping around the room. There's a logbook that's seen better days, a chest full of clothes that I will *not* be touching, and... "There we go." A wickedly curved knife that will do the trick in a pinch.

I've just turned for the door when a cry goes up among the crew. I recognize the panic. It's the same I heard the last time Maura came to port in Ashye. Or tried to. I watched from the castle with my heart in my throat as her ship was driven away by the navy. We were both nineteen, and she'd created that reputation she'd always wanted, a young pirate captain so fearsome that ships would surrender without a fight. Not someone my father wanted in his city...or around his daughter.

She never tried to come back.

Surely she hasn't made it here this fast, though. It seems to defy belief. Staying put is the smartest thing to do, but curiosity has its hold in me, and I can't resist trying to catch a glimpse. With how my luck is going, it's just as likely that it's some other pirate who's taken exception to the dear captain and decided to do what pirates do.

Or worse...my father has sent the royal navy after me.

I hoist my bag over my shoulder and crack open the cabin door. Shouts and pounding feet greet my ears, but I can't see anything properly without going out onto deck. At least the captain is nowhere in evidence, but that doesn't really mean anything. He's close. He has to be.

I yank the door all the way open. No point in trying to be sneaky; as soon as I breach the narrow doorway, everyone will see me. I drag in a breath and charge forward...only to stop short when I get a good look around.

It seems like only minutes since the captain chained me to his desk, but apparently more time than I realized has passed. The shore is a smudge in the distance, much too far away for me to swim, even if I were a strong swimmer. I'm not. "Shit," I breathe.

The ship jerks to a stop.

It happens so suddenly, I stagger a few steps forward. The crew cries out in fear and then anger as everyone rushes to the left side of the ship. *What's going on?* But I know, don't I? Maura is here. She's come for me.

"Where is she?"

Even over the wind and other sounds, even with so many years and far too much baggage between us, I would know Maura's voice anywhere. My throat tries to close, and I rush forward, elbowing my way through the crew to get to the side of the ship.

And there she is, standing on the railing, one hand on a rope to steady her, with her long blonde hair whipping in the wind. *Maura.*

I must say it aloud, because the crew starts to realize I'm among them. They curse and jump back as if I have some sort of contagious disease. The captain is the only one who doesn't. He glares at me. "You didn't mention you were bound for *The Kelpie.*"

"You didn't ask," I say primly. "I'll be going now."

He looks like he wants to argue, but with the crew muttering around him and making the sign to ward against evil, he doesn't have much of a choice. He spits at my feet. "Get off my ship."

"Happily." I turn for the railing, only to pause. "Um, how?"

"You want her?" The captain's voice becomes a roar. "Well, then go get her." He shoves me.

My hips catch the railing, and for a moment, I think it will be fine, but he shoves my shoulders again, and then I am very much *not* fine. I tip over the railing and fall.

It's a longer fall than I expected. I have a moment to realize why the crew members were so scared before I hit the water.

Maura somehow lifted their entire ship into the air.

2

MAURA

"Damn it!" I spin, but my quartermaster, Cai, is already shoving the other ship away, zir expression a mask of concentration as ze uses zir power to ensure Juliette doesn't get crushed between us.

Having a full-blown firefight within eyesight of Ashye is the height of foolishness, especially with the crown princess in the mix, but as Juliette hits the water hard enough to make me flinch, I find I don't give a fuck. "Sink them."

"Captain?"

"You heard me." I shrug out of my coat and dive into the water. We're closer to the surface than *The Drowning Maid*, since Cai's air magic is holding them aloft. Ze will have to rest after getting us here and dealing with the confrontation, but that's fine. I have half a dozen air mages on the crew for a reason.

I catch sight of Juliette below me. She's frantically flailing her arms and legs, but it's not making a difference. She's sinking as if someone tied an anchor to her. I curse, letting loose a string of bubbles, and add a bit of my own magic to the mix, using it to increase my speed.

Seconds later, I have my arms around her waist. Even as worried as I am about her drowning, I can't help but notice how soft she is. Gods, but I missed her.

I can't think like that, though.

No matter what we shared as kids...as teens...I know all too well how foolish it is to hope for something that can never be. Juliette is the *crown princess*. And I am quite possibly her father's biggest frustration because of how many of his shipments I've lifted before they reached his port.

It's harder than it should be to get us to the surface. Juliette's bag is too damn heavy, but when I try to pull it off her, she fights me. We don't have time for this nonsense. I can hold my breath for a significant amount of time. She can't.

I send a surge of magic downward, propelling us toward the surface. We break through to precious air. A wave of heat that makes my skin prickle slaps me in the face. Juliette cries out, but I'm already moving, towing her away from the flaming ruins of the *Maid* and toward *The Kelpie*. My crew did what I demanded. Even as we swim, fireballs shoot overhead, ensuring there's nothing left of *The Drowning Maid*.

The rope ladder descends, and I see Cai's exhausted face over the top of the railing. There will be no convenient trip to the deck from zir with Cai as tired as zir must be. I grab the bottom of the rope ladder and hook my arm through it. "Can you climb?"

"Of course." Juliette is shaking like a leaf, and her lower lip is trembling, though I can't begin to guess if it's fear or the temperature. It's not as cold as it gets in the winter, but that doesn't change the fact that it's significantly cooler than the balmy afternoon air.

I glare. "You're lying."

"I'm not." She tries for a smile. "After you."

If I climb this ladder, she's liable to fall back into the water and sink to the bottom before I realize what's happening. "Not a chance." I flick out an impatient hand. "Give me your bag." Her pampered princess life shows in every line of her soft body, which I am *certainly* not eyeing as she curses and starts climbing.

Definitely not.

Her pale purple dress clings to her wide hips and thick thighs and... Gods, her ass makes my mouth water. As she climbs, I catch myself watching the crease at the bottom curve of her rear, where her thighs meet—

Pull yourself together.

I shake my head and ascend after her. I almost have myself under control by the time I reach the deck. At least until Juliette turns to me and I realize the front of her dress is now just as sheer at the back. I can clearly see her breasts—her *nipples*—through the fabric, and her soft stomach, and her...

Cai clears zir throat. "Captain—"

"A moment." I scoop up my coat and drape it over Juliette's shoulders. "This will serve well enough until we get you back to Ashye."

She clutches the jacket around her, but there's a stubborn tilt to her chin that I don't like. "I'm not going back."

Surely she did not say what I think she just said. "Excuse me?"

"I'm not going back," she repeats deliberately.

I glance at my crew, which is watching this exchange with undisguised interest. Even Cai, who's obviously fighting not to slump against the mast. The king of Skoiya is no friend of ours. We took a risk in coming this close to the port where he and the royal navy reside, especially after they almost sank us the last time we tried. We can't linger.

"I don't know what game of pretend you're playing at, but we aren't kids anymore." I keep my voice low, pitched to carry only as far as Juliette. We may both be significantly changed since we saw each other last, but some things don't shift with the years, and I suspect her pride is one of those things. If I push too hard, she'll dig in her heels out of sheer perversity. "Your presence on this ship has real-life consequences to me and my crew. You could get us killed."

"As if you're not the most feared pirate crew in this part of the world." Her full lips curve, though her dark eyes are bittersweet. "You did what you set out to do."

We are *not* having this conversation right now. Maybe not ever. I turn to Cai. "Set our course for the next port south. We'll book her passage home from there." I won't ever sail into Ashye again. Not even for Juliette.

Cai nods and heads to the helm. I sweep a look over the rest of my crew. Most of them have sailed with me for the better part of a decade. I know them as well as the back of my hand, and right now they're looking at Juliette like she's a particularly tasty morsel.

She *is*, but that's beside the point.

"You have places to be." I don't have to raise my voice much; the snap in it gets them moving. I wait a beat to ensure everything is as it should be and then grab Juliette's arm. "My cabin. Now."

"Already taking me to your room. Maura, how forward." Her teasing lilt doesn't quite cover the way she's shaking.

It makes me want to strip her out of her wet clothes and tuck her into my bed, but I can't afford to do that. Having her in my coat is headfuck enough. She's not mine. The fool who believed she could be died out on these seas a long time ago. I'm a different person now. "Let's go."

Even though I tell myself we don't know each other anymore, I can't help watching her take in my ship and crew as we walk up the stairs to the captain's quarters. No, that's a lie. I'm flat-out watching *her*. She looks good, her warm-brown skin glowing with health, her long dark hair wet down her back so it doesn't show the waves I used to run my fingers through. She's cut it, so it reaches just past her shoulders instead of most of the way down her back.

Juliette doesn't speak until we step into the cabin and I shut the door firmly. She smiles sweetly. "You really did it, didn't you? A ship of your own. A crew that looks at you like the sun rises and sets at your command."

Despite everything, I flush, though I can't begin to say if it's in embarrassment or pride. "Those were the dreams spun by a foolish girl." Once upon a time, we used to hide on the roof of the old inn near the docks and wait for shooting stars so we could make wishes.

I wish to be the greatest pirate captain the world has ever known.

Well, I wish to sail at your side and go on many grand adventures.

Where would you go, Juliette?

It doesn't matter as long as I'm with you.

Except that was the most impossible wish of all. That a princess could ever have a life with a penniless orphan, even after that orphan became a pirate captain to strike fear into the hearts of men. We were so *young*. We thought if we just wished hard enough, the world would bend to our wills.

"And yet your wish came true." She turns slowly, surveying my quarters.

I try to see it through her eyes. It's roomier than the space most of my crew has, but I made changes to the ship the moment I had the resources for it, so it's about a third of the size it used to be. The other two thirds are now designated for Cai as my quartermaster and Daichi as my navigator. I've outfitted the space as comfortably as possible. There is a small bookshelf filled with a selection of books that I change up every time we reach port, a magical navigating table that Daichi insisted we invest in and that I've never regretted, a desk, and my bed.

Best not to think about the last.

"You can get cleaned up in here." I open the door to the bathroom I share with the other two. Another upgrade the last captain hadn't bothered with but that was nonnegotiable for me. The crew has its own bathroom belowdecks as well. It costs a pretty penny to keep a special water reserve for bathing, but we all agree that it's worth it.

Juliette pokes her head in and turns to me, brows raised. "Is this a normal thing for a pirate ship?"

Again, that flush of not quite embarrassment. I look away. "I already live in close quarters with the others for weeks at a time. No reason for us to stink, too."

She laughs softly. "I think the captain of *The Drowning Maid* could take notes."

I'm still processing that she's *here*. Not hidden away in her castle. Not walking down the aisle to some foreign dignitary. Not training to rule Skoiya after her bastard of a father is gone.

Here. In my quarters. My ring still on her finger.

"Are you okay?"

She gives me a surprised look. "Of course. Why wouldn't I be?"

"I can think of a few reasons." I hold up my fingers as I list each one. "You were kidnapped. You almost drowned. Now I'm taking you away from your home, even if you will be returned there."

"Oh." She blinks. "Well, to the first point, he didn't kidnap me. Or at least, he didn't initially do it. I kidnapped myself." She makes a face. "But then the kidnapping became far too real, which is why I called for help."

That's a lot to process. Again, I wonder if I misheard her, but I couldn't possibly have. "You kidnapped...yourself."

"Well, yes." She tucks her hair behind her ears. "I waited for six months past the agreed-upon date, but you never came, and it occurred to me that it wasn't fair to ask you to do all the work."

Her words strike right to the very heart of me. I can't pretend I don't remember the promises we made at sixteen. It was ten years ago, but it might as well have been yesterday.

Promise me, Maura. Promise me he won't win. Promise me we'll be together.

I promise, Juliette.

I'm a godsdamned liar. But then, so is she.

"That was a long time ago," I finally manage.

"Well, yes, but..." Her smile dims. "Oh, I see. You don't mean it fondly. You mean you never meant to honor that promise."

3

JULIETTE

My father was right.

I hate that my first thought feels like a betrayal of Maura. I hate that I'm standing here, smiling like the worst kind of fool, while she stands there looking sick and vaguely guilty.

Even with that expression on her face, she's still the most stunning woman I've ever seen. Her skin is a few shades darker than when we were together, no doubt courtesy of living outside in the sun every day, and her blonde hair is a few shades lighter. She's got new scars, too. There's a scattering of burn marks along her hairline, as if someone threw embers at her face, and a silver mark that starts at the corner of her mouth and curves down past her chin.

Her wet clothes are plastered to her athletic body, her lean muscles on full display in a way that would make my heart beat harder if it weren't in the process of breaking.

"You were never going to come for me," I say slowly, testing the words out. "You lied."

"It wasn't a lie when I said it all those years ago."

Somehow, that just makes it worse. "Is there someone else?"

She jerks back like I struck her. "Juliette, we were *sixteen* when we made that promise. Don't pretend like you've been celibate and waiting for me these past ten years. I may be on your father's Most Wanted list, but I still hear things coming out of Ashye. You're the social darling of a nation, and your list of paramours is as long as my arm."

I set my chin, refusing to feel guilty. "Oh, because you've been waiting for me all these years?"

"It's complicated. But to answer your question—no, there's no one else. It's not like that."

"Then what *is* it like? Because I'm having a hard time understanding." Gods, I hate how my voice gets choked. It feels like she reached through time and distance to stab the dreaming girl I used to be. "Just tell me why. I deserve that much."

Maura sucks in a breath. She's not looking at me, and it's a relief and an agony all at the same time. "We're from different worlds. Maybe that didn't seem like an insurmountable obstacle when we were sixteen, but we're not sixteen anymore, Juliette. You are the *crown princess*, and I am a pirate your father has spent significant time and resources trying to catch so he can hang me. We are not the same."

"I'm not."

"That's what I just—"

"No, that's not what I mean." I shake my head. "I'm not the crown princess anymore. My father deemed me too irresponsible to be trusted with the throne, so he's passed me over for my cousin Drake."

Maura finally looks at me, but I almost wish she hadn't because of the pity in her green eyes. "I'm sorry. I hadn't heard."

It's been months since the announcement was made, and while part of me wants to give her the benefit of the doubt, the truth is that rumors run across the sea just as fast as in the city. If she didn't know, it means she hasn't been seeking out any crumb of information about me the way I have with her.

Which means she likely doesn't know my father had every intention of shipping me off to the sticky heat of the north to marry the monarch of Edrines. That, more than anything, is what spurred me to go looking for Maura. There is no coastline in Edrines. If I moved there, any hope of a future where she came for me would be gone for good.

Except apparently she never had any intention of coming for me at all.

"You tried to reach the port when we were nineteen. Just three years after you left."

She's still watching me with too much and too little in her eyes. "I was still young enough then to think I was immortal. I almost got my entire crew killed as a result."

There's no reason to think a future with me should outweigh the lives of so many. But that's an excuse and we both know it. There are other ways into the city that don't involve sailing into the bay. She didn't come because she didn't want to.

I shrug out of her jacket and hold it out. "Well, this is suitably embarrassing. You don't need to drop me off at the next port south. I can find my way from here."

Maura lifts a brow. I've always been so damned jealous she can do that. When I was younger, I used to practice in the mirror to attempt to replicate it, but I've never managed. She crosses her arms over her chest, and I'm only human. Of course, I look at the way the motion makes her white shirt cling to her chest. Her breasts are smaller than mine but absolutely perfect in every way. I can clearly see her rosy nipples through the fabric.

My body gives a pulse of desire that I try very hard to ignore. "Why are you looking at me like that?" I snap.

"We're at sea. How in the gods' names do you expect to find your own way from here?"

I open my mouth to tell her I have a piece of eight that will grant me access to Atlantis, but I stop before the words escape.

If she's done with me, then she's done with me. There's no reason to tell her more than I already have. "That's my concern."

"Juliette." She sighs. "You were kidnapped and had to call for help within a few hours of leaving port. Surely you can see that it's not wise to make a go of it alone. No matter how capable you think you are, you've spent your entire life in a gilded palace where there were servants to take care of your every whim. It's not like that out here."

Of course it's not. I may be a bit naive at times, but I'm not actually a fool... Or at least I didn't think I was until today. Now I'm not so sure.

No.

Damn it, *no.*

I will not doubt myself. Not now. Not ever.

"You've made your thoughts on me very clear. I thank you for your help, but that's where this ends." It's on the tip of my tongue to ask her why she bothered to rescue me when she obviously wants nothing to do with me, but my pride won't let me ask the question. "I'll just clean up now." I reach for my bag, which is still slung over her shoulder.

Maura steps back out of reach. "Don't do that."

"Don't do what?"

She rolls her eyes, and it's so purely Maura that my heart ripples with pain. "Don't get all pissy with me for pointing out the obvious. I'm trying to help."

"I don't need your help."

She snorts. "Right, because you were doing so well alone on *The Drowning Maid.* That's why you called for *my* help."

I reach for the bag again, and again she shifts back. "What do you *want,* Maura? You say there's nothing here for me, but you're not exactly letting me leave right now."

"I just want to help." She almost sounds like she means it. She bites her bottom lip, the gesture harkening back to our younger selves. How can so much have changed and yet she be so familiar to me? She lifts a hand, her knuckles scarred with silver lines. "Hold still."

I don't have time to protest, not that I'd bother. I'm wet and cold and hurt in a way that has nothing to do with the physical. If she wants to dry my clothes, then I'm not going to stop her.

It's very strange to watch her pull the water from the fabric and my hair. Elementals are relatively rare, at least in Skoiya. Maybe because my father looks down on that magic, calling it unsophisticated. He prefers magic that comes from pomp and ritual. I have no magic at all, so I'm even below the elementals in his eyes.

Maura flicks her wrist, and the water gathered in the air between us shoots out the window near the desk. "There."

"That wasn't necessary."

"Juliette." Her smile is sad and a little sweet. "You're welcome." She hands over my bag. "I have to speak with my people, but take as much time as you need. It will be a day or two before we reach our destination."

I blink. "It takes a week to reach Oplain."

Maura's smile goes fierce, her teeth white against her tanned skin. "Maybe for normal folks. I have a dozen elementals who specialize in air on my crew. The winds are always with us."

So eager to be rid of me.

I don't say it. I gave up begging for the people in my life to love me a long time ago. I never thought I'd have to beg *Maura*, but that just goes to show that even the most unexpected person can let you down. "I see."

"We'll talk soon." She turns and walks out of the cabin without another word, and it's just as well. I'm not sure what I'd even say.

It seems we are different people entirely from the kids who met so long ago. I'd snuck away from my tutor, a naive soul who thought getting out to see how normal people lived would season me as a ruler. Xe didn't last three months before my father found out and fired xem, but by then it was too late. I'd already met Maura and learned how to slip from the castle grounds.

I still remember my first sight of her, skinny and dirty and slipping between the taller adults in the crowd like a fish slips around rocks in a stream.

She stole my bracelet that day.

I met with her six times in the next few months to convince her to give it back, until it became a ritual that bonded us. I just wanted more time with her.

Take this amulet and give me my bracelet back.

That amulet is old and rusty. Pass.

Okay, then how about my dress?

What am I going to do with that dress, Princess? I'll be hanged as a thief the moment I try to pawn it.

As time passed and we grew older, we never quite gave up that game. It hurts to remember how I felt every time I offered something new and more extravagant and impossible. It hurts even more to know how it ended, almost a year to the day after we started that ritual.

I'll trade you the moon for my bracelet, Maura. Surely that's a fair balance.

I can hardly carry around the moon in my pocket. And all the stars would get jealous. That's a curse for someone who wants to navigate by them someday.

Well... What about a kiss?

A kiss?

Yes, a kiss. I'll trade you a kiss for the bracelet.

It was my first kiss. My best kiss, even, because of how twisted up the whole experience made me. Even more so when Maura slipped my bracelet back into my hand afterward. I honestly hadn't thought she'd kept it.

Before I left that day, I slipped it right back into her bag when she wasn't looking.

I glance out the window just as the remains of *The Drowning Maid* disappear beneath the waves. An entire crew, gone at the command of the girl who traded a bracelet for a kiss. Granted, who knows what they were going to do with me, in general and once we got out to sea, but that's a lot of what-if. What Maura did is very much real.

I know she has a fearsome reputation, of course. She's not at the top of the list of people my father would like to hang simply because she and I lost our innocence to each other ten years ago...and were subsequently caught by my maid at the time.

Maura is a villain to the people of Skoiya.

I just never expected her to be a villain to me, too.

4

MAURA

Getting the water out of my clothes and hair only does so much. The fabric is now stiff with dried salt, and my hair has seen better days. Not that I have reason to care how I look. I don't. I meant what I said to Juliette. I have every intention of putting her in a carriage home the first chance I get.

I'm not sure how I'll guarantee her safety, though.

Highwaymen haunt the roads the same way I haunt the seas. Not to mention there's nothing stopping Juliette from getting into all sorts of trouble without someone to look after her. She's always been like that, always ready to dive into a situation without any thought to the danger involved. I don't know if it's a byproduct of being a pampered princess or if it's just her, but it was a full-time job keeping her out of trouble when we were kids. It was like the dangers of the city just never occurred to her. Like she believed she was untouchable.

I can't imagine that's changed.

Cai stands at the helm. Ze looks steadier, zir dark brown skin less waxy. I move to stand next to zir. "Update me."

Ze shakes zir head. "So we're not going to talk about how

you scorched that ship to the bottom of the sea despite them not opening fire on us?"

I level a look at zir that would send most new recruits scurrying away, but Cai has been with me since the beginning. We joined our first crew at the same time and worked our way to the top. Ze knows me better than anyone, which means there's no way to avoid the question even though ze already knows the answer. "You're going to make me say it, aren't you?"

"Yep."

I stare out across the water for a moment. "She's not really mine, not in any way that matters, but that doesn't change the fact they took someone who's mine and had to pay the price."

"Mm-hmm." Cai makes a minute adjustment to our course. "And if she's yours enough for us to raze another ship and crew, why exactly are we delivering her back to land?"

Because Juliette *isn't* mine. She never was, and she never can be. "You know what will happen if he sends the royal navy after us."

"He's tried it before."

"It was different before. He wants me dead, but he knows he has time since we don't raid villages on the coastline like some of the others. If he finds out we took his only daughter, he'll rally the entirety of his force against us."

Cai shrugs. "So maybe he doesn't find out."

I give zir a sharp look. "People talk, and Juliette doesn't exactly blend in. First port we make, whispers will start, and it will only be a matter of time before they get back to her father."

"So you *did* think about it." Ze gives me a triumphant grin. "I knew it."

I open my mouth, pause, and glare. "I have a responsibility to the crew. Putting them in danger for my personal desires will get me voted out."

"You've made the crew rich beyond their wildest dreams, and you've invested a fortune in *The Kelpie* to make things downright luxurious. You'd have to start murdering them one by one, and even then it would take some time for the rest to turn on you."

If the royal navy came after us, being murdered by me would be a mercy. Death by hanging is a bad enough end, but no doubt we wouldn't get there quickly. The king's pet executioner has a reputation for torturing his captives for days... sometimes weeks.

I shudder. "No. It's too risky."

"To us...or to your heart?"

I'm saved from answering by Juliette walking out onto the deck. I tense as her gaze sweeps over me, but she turns away and walks to the railing. It takes less than thirty seconds for her to start drawing people in. The crew knows better than to get too close, but Daichi gives me a smirk and leans against the railing at Juliette's side.

He says something to make her laugh, and the sound races across the distance between us to burrow right into my chest. Gods, but she looks even better now that she's cleaned up than she did straight out of the sea. Her wavy black hair falls to her shoulders in waves I want to dig my hands into. Even stiffened by the salt of the water, her dress is far more luxurious than anything else on this ship. It's also more risqué than what's in fashion in court right now, the fabric clinging to her breasts and stomach and hips.

Even as I watch, Daichi leans closer and rakes a charming look over Juliette, earning another laugh. What is he saying?

"Keep grinding your teeth like that, and there won't be much in the way of teeth left."

"Shut up," I mutter without taking my eyes off the pair. It's only because I'm watching so closely that I see Juliette cast a sly glance in my direction and then place a hand against Daichi's chest.

I'm moving before I make a conscious decision to, bounding

down the stairs and stopping in front of them. "Daichi, you have somewhere to be."

His grin widens just a bit. If I thought for a second there were harm in him, I'd toss him overboard and...

What am I saying?

Daichi has sailed with me for three years. He's one of the best navigators I've ever worked with. The crew adores him, and his charm and humor—and skill at telling stories—make a world of difference on longer voyages. He's one of mine, yet I'm standing here, truly considering painting the deck red with his blood. "Go."

His grin dies at the sharpness in my tone, and he jerks straight. "Yes, Captain."

Juliette barely waits for him to move away to spin on me. "Are you serious right now?"

"Keep your voice down." In seven years as a captain, I've only lost my reason a handful of times, and only under the most extreme of circumstances. This is not that, no matter what my instincts are telling me. "You will not undermine me in front of my crew."

She tosses up her hands and makes a sound that's pure frustration. "For gods' sake, Maura, what do you want from me? It's certainly not *me*, so if you could loop me in, I would— Ack!"

I grab her arm and haul her behind me back to the cabin. Even as I do, some part of my mind demands to know what the fuck I think I'm doing. That voice has kept me alive over the years, but right now it's drowned out by pure frustration.

I slam the door behind us and whirl around to face her. Now's the time to say something, to crush the possibility of a future between a fugitive and a princess of the realm once and for all. The words are right there on the tip of my tongue, the precise phrase to shatter us.

But Juliette is so damned beautiful in her fury, her dark eyes sparking and her full lips parted to deliver what will no doubt be a cutting remark.

It's not even a matter of choice.

I need to kiss her more than I need the sun on my face and the rolling deck of my ship beneath my feet.

So I do.

I hook the back of her neck and pull her against me. She's so fucking *soft*, it drives me wild, especially when she makes a furious sound against my lips and digs her hands into my hair, dragging me closer.

It's strange how so much can change and yet this hasn't. I memorized the taste of her, even with so many years between us, memorized the feel of her body giving against mine, the little sounds she makes as she tries to writhe closer.

That reasonable voice in the back of my mind is screaming to stop this immediately, but I'm not listening. Juliette is the north wind, sweeping away all else before her.

We stumble toward my bed in a tangle of limbs and grasping hands. She yanks off my shirt, and I manage to get her dress down past her breasts before I'm distracted by their perfection, the curve of them begging for my mouth, her brown nipples tight and needing my tongue. "Juliette."

"Don't you dare say something to ruin this."

I manage a choked laugh. Any thought of reason, of regrets, is drowning in a sea of desire. "Take off your clothes."

"Only if you get rid of those pants." She glares at my pants as if they've insulted her personally. With how hard they are to get off, perhaps they have. "Now, Maura. We can fight later. I missed you too much."

Again, reason tries to interject, to demand I stop this before my body makes promises that I have no intention of following through on. Again, I ignore it.

Juliette doesn't actually let me get my pants all the way off before she shoves me back onto the bed. I still have one boot on, and my pants are stuck around my calf, but I couldn't give a fuck when her mouth is on mine and her bare skin is pressing against me.

"I am so angry at you," she murmurs against my throat.

"The feeling is—"

She nips the curve of my breast and then sucks my nipple into her mouth. Hard. What was I saying? I can't think, can't speak. "More."

"You are *such* an asshole." She delves one hand between my thighs and cups my pussy. Despite her harsh words, her breath shudders out in time with mine.

That gets me moving. I grab her hips and pull her up and over until she's straddling one of my thighs and I'm doing the same to hers. I can't get over how soft her skin is. Not weathered from the sun and air and water. Not scarred from far more fights than a single person can remember. Untouched by all the harsher elements the world brings to the fore.

I grip her big ass and urge her to grind on me. I want to touch her, to taste her, to inhale every bit of this experience so I can tuck it away for when it's gone forever. The greediness of my desire isn't new.

It's always been like this with Juliette.

She's someone I was never meant to have, and the thief in me, the hunter in me, cannot resist marring her perfection with my bloodstained hands.

No matter where she goes, whom she inevitably marries, no matter how gilded and perfect her life, she will always carry the imprint of my fingers, my mouth, my words.

I really am the villain her father named me.

5

JULIETTE

Maura kisses me like she always has. Like she wants to ruin me for all others. I'll never tell her the truth, that she accomplished that goal when we were sixteen and virgins, fumbling at each other's clothes and laughing in the giddy way that only seems to come with first love.

Or maybe it only comes with this woman.

I *hate* that. She wants to ruin me, but I want to ruin her right back. *She* left me and had no intention of keeping her promise. *She* is determined to drop me at the nearest port and wash her hands of me for good.

Fine. So be it.

But I'll make her regret it. I'll make her miss me...even if she'll never admit it aloud.

I ignore her sound of protest and slide down her body. The bed is a strange contraption that is almost like a hammock but with more structure. It sways as I move, and I have the distant thought that the movement could be really interesting for bedroom games before I get distracted parting Maura's thighs.

She's a marvel. It's honestly upsetting. She had a few scars even when we were teenagers, but she's covered in them now. They slice down her toned stomach and pucker the skin at her hip and thigh. There are even two jagged spots on her other thigh from magical weapons, the flesh obviously seared on contact.

She's almost died. *Many* times.

The thought tries to close my throat, but I can't let myself demand explanations. What's the point? She's a pirate, and piracy is a dangerous life.

Her body is much paler than her face and arms and chest. Seeing her like this feels like a secret just between us. I can't afford to think like that, not when she's so blatantly planning to dump me off her ship at the first opportunity. But I'm only human, and I've been in love with Maura for most of my life. If I can only have her right now, like this, then I'll take what I can get.

I slide down her body as well as I can in the relatively cramped space and press a kiss to her lower stomach. I've had lovers that I teased for hours, seeing just how far I could push them, but this is *Maura*. If I don't get my mouth on her properly, I might expire on the spot.

The first taste of her goes straight to my head. She gives a surprisingly sweet whimper as I lick her pussy, and I suddenly need to do whatever it takes to inspire that sound again.

To make her cry out *my* name.

In the ten years since those first fumbling attempts at love-making, I've learned plenty. I know how to make my lovers shake and squirm and orgasm so hard, it alters their world-views. I've felt selfish pride at the way many of them linger at the edges of my presence, desperate for another experience in my bed.

All that poise and cunning abandon me at my second taste. Maura's pussy goes to my head faster than fine wine. I press her thighs wide and cover her with my mouth. During those months we shared before my father drove her out, I learned this woman's body as well as my own.

She's different now. We both are.

I mean to relearn it, even if this is only happening a single time.

Maura digs her hands into my hair and lifts her hips. "Gods, Juliette. That feels good."

I have to fight to lift my head, to break the contact of my tongue against her clit. "Say it again." I hardly sound like myself. That's fine. I don't feel much like myself right now, either. "Say my name again."

Her laugh is hoarse with pleasure. "Getting possessive?"

With her? Always. I know better than to admit as much, though. Instead I ease a finger into her pussy. She gasps and arches her back, putting her small breasts on display. It's not fair how beautiful she is, how much I want her.

Mine.

Except she's not.

My throat tries to close, but I push the thought away just like I've pushed away thoughts of Maura over the years. Court is rife with intrigue, and it was vital everyone assumed I forgot about my youthful indiscretion. If they thought I was still pining after the pirate my father wanted in the noose, they would have used the information to pry right into the heart of me. The only time I allowed myself to think of Maura was when I was truly alone.

I stroke her clit with my tongue and work another finger into her. I might have forgotten so much, but I haven't forgotten *this*. I twist my wrist and find that spot that makes her...

"Holy *fuck*, Juliette."

Yes. That.

Her grip tightens in my hair, urging my face harder against her pussy. I nearly purr in bliss. This. This is how it's supposed to be: her riding my mouth and fingers to orgasm, her ragged breathing and little moans filling the cabin.

Now that we're like this, I can almost believe that nothing's changed. That this can last until the end of time. What place does reality have in the slickness of Maura's pussy on my tongue and her fingers digging into my hair?

I could do this forever. I want to do this forever.

"Juliette!" She arches her back, and her thighs clamp around my head. "Don't stop! Oh my gods, please don't stop."

She's not thinking about all the reasons we can't be together right now. She's only thinking about me. If I don't stop, this will be over too soon, and then Maura will get back to telling me all the reasons this will never work. Instead of keeping my pace steady in a way I know will get her over the edge, I slow. I lick around her clit, depriving her of the touch she needs to finish. I stop the rhythmic motions of my fingers inside her, giving her the penetration but not the friction.

In response, Maura whimpers. It's such a sweet sound, nothing like the woman I knew then or have interacted with now. And yet I don't want to stop. I don't want to tease her and make her beg. I want to keep going until she comes apart around me, until all she thinks about is *me*.

I've just decided that this game of drawing things out is silly and I don't want to do it anymore when Maura digs her fingers even harder into my hair and drags me up her body. "I don't remember you being such a tease," she growls against my mouth.

"Maybe I've learned some patience in the past ten years."

"We both know that's not true."

She's not wrong. I grin even though my chest aches at the reminder of all the time apart. "Okay, that isn't true at all. But I *have* learned a trick or two since I last shared your bed." Not that we often ended up in a bed. Our time together was too scarce, riddled with the threat of being a caught. We were both sneaking out to meet each other, and while I technically had money, Maura wouldn't let me spend it on something that might bring attention to us. Like a room at an inn.

But if one thing is true, it's that her patience has never been her strong suit either. I have a bare moment, maybe two, before she takes control. I need her to orgasm before that happens. I stop fucking around and descend to suck her clit into my mouth, using the flat of my tongue against the underside the way that she used to love.

She cries out, and I know I have her. Her pussy clamps around my fingers, and her hands tighten in my hair until I'm distantly worried that she might rip out a chunk.

The moment passes far too quickly. She curses and slumps back to the bed.

I can't help giving her one last long lick. It breaks my heart that I'll never have my mouth on her pussy again, but this is goodbye.

I start to sit up when she curses. "Oh, no, you don't." She flips us before I have a chance to formulate a response. She pins me to the bed, and even though under Maura is exactly where I want to be, I can't help but struggle. It feels like no matter what I do, I am never actually in control. That might be a relief if I could trust her to have my best interests at heart, but I'm not that naive.

She wants me gone, and if this moment right now between us means anything, it only means the end.

Her hands close around my wrists, and she presses them more firmly against the bed. She wedges one leg between mine and uses her hips to keep me in place. It has the bonus of pressing her tightly to my pussy. Every time I try to throw her off, delicious friction sends ripples of pleasure through me. To the point where I'm not sure if I'm actually even fighting her anymore or just rubbing myself wantonly against her thigh.

"I hate you!"

"Do you?" Maura sets her teeth to the sensitive skin of my throat. "Or are you just angry because I won't let you keep the upper hand?"

Yes. No. I don't know. Nothing about this has gone like I expected, not from the moment I orchestrated my own kidnapping to right now, with each movement driving my need higher.

I don't want to give her the satisfaction of making me orgasm, but I don't think I have a choice. Not with her releasing one of my wrists to hook my leg and guide it around her waist. She uses her hips to urge me into a rhythm that makes my heart stutter.

The moment I realize I'm in danger, it's too late. My body goes tight and hot, the wave cresting over me and pulling me under until I am nothing more than a body with needs. Maura, the bastard, kisses me the very same sweet way she used to, even as she grabs my hips and grinds me harder against her thigh. She keeps my orgasm rising and rising, and just when it's about to crest again, she slides down my body and presses her mouth to my pussy.

The soft slickness of her tongue is a direct counterpoint to how firm her thigh was. A second ago, I would've sworn I was too sensitive to keep going, but now I dig my hands into her hair and hold her to me.

Not that she needs encouragement. She licks and sucks and teases me with a frenzy that I am foolish enough to hope means she missed me too. I won't ask. I may be a fool, but I still have my pride.

"Come for me, Jules. I want to taste it." Maura works two fingers into me and angles them so she can stroke her fingertips against that deliciously sensitive spot inside me. Combined with her tongue and my earlier orgasm, I don't stand a chance of holding out. At this point I'm not even trying to; I'm simply along for the ride.

I hate that she still knows my body so well. I hate how good this feels. But most of all, I hate how much it's going to hurt when it's over. There's a reason I've never indulged in goodbye sex before. It's messy, and no matter how decadent things are in the moment, with heightened emotions, the crash landing hurts all the more when it's through.

I don't know how I'll recover from this, but that's a worry for a future Juliette. Right now, all I'm capable of is clinging to Maura as she plays my body to a tune of her own making.

6

JULIETTE

I wake up alone.

It's nothing more than I expected, but with my body still aching from good sex and Maura's sea scent lingering on my skin, I'm having a hard time remembering that. I stare at the wooden ceiling overhead, the bed swinging gently as the ship cuts through the waves.

No matter what Maura believes, I'm not naive. I know her life is dangerous and that ten years can change a person until they're a complete stranger. I'm not the same sweet girl she knew back then, but I don't think she's noticed. No reason for that to feel like a direct attack, but it does.

I knew going in that it would be a long shot to convince her that we could have something. Maybe I didn't admit it to myself until right now, but the fear lingered in the back of my mind despite the hope I stubbornly clung to.

No longer.

It's time for plan B.

I'm not going back to the castle. When my father first began entertaining an alliance with the monarch of Edrines, I took the liberty of looking into them myself. They're sixty and have twelve children my age and older. Even if they're not a monster —and, by all accounts, they seem fair enough—their children would not take kindly to another marriage bringing the potential for more rivals to the throne. The politics in Edrines make my father's court look like a playground. I'd be killed within six months.

I happen to like living, and I've already been passed over for my own throne. The only way to ensure I can make my own choices is to get as far from Skoiya as possible. Maura has managed to avoid my father's grasp for years, so I thought she'd be a good option, but if she's determined to see the back of me... It doesn't matter. I had a plan to reach Atlantis, and there's no reason to change it just because Maura doesn't want me.

It takes only a few minutes to get dressed. My gown is stiff and itchy, but the second gown I brought is no better. It's fine. There will be plenty of options where I'm headed. I just need to get there.

The piece of eight is exactly where I hid it, sewn into the bodice of my lilac gown. I couldn't risk its loss if I were separated from my bag for some reason. There's a jewel-encrusted dagger on Maura's desk with a wickedly sharp point that makes quick work of my sloppy stitches.

The piece of eight doesn't look like much. If I didn't know the magic attached to it, I might have written it off as some archaic coin that's all but worthless. I suppose that's part of its mystique. It's not a coin at all.

It's a key.

It warms against my palm, and I take a long, slow breath. If I do this, there's no going back. I'll be truly on my own in a way I've never experienced. No father to threaten my enemies with. No Maura to swoop in and save me.

Where I'm going, she won't be able to reach me. No one will.

I sling my bag over my shoulder and take a fortifying

breath. Every other time I've said goodbye to Maura, it's been with the promise of seeing her again in the future. That won't be the case this time. It's goodbye for good. I tighten my hold on the piece of eight until its edges dig into my palm.

No reason to wait. The longer I stand here, the easier it will be to talk myself out of taking this step. I won't pretend I'm not scared, but I haven't let fear stop me up to this point, and I'm not going to let it stop me now.

The first fingers of dawn stretch across the sky as I step out of the cabin and onto the deck. The fear I am most firmly *not* feeling tries to take hold, but I catch sight of the coastline in the distance. If I don't move now, I won't have another chance.

There are two people standing on either side of the mast, moving in slow motions that draw the wind to them and direct it into the sail. I watch for a few moments, marveling at their control. It must be a challenging balance to siphon exactly as much as they need. Not too much, which might rip the mast right off, and not too little, which would exhaust the elemental user unnecessarily. Maura really has gathered the best around her.

I find the woman herself at the helm. She's changed into another set of what she was wearing yesterday—a loose white shirt with a deep V that gives a hint of her chest and a pair of fitted pants tucked into boots. She even has on the long black jacket that seems like it should be much too warm for the time of year, but I suppose it keeps her dry.

I very pointedly don't look at her chest, at the line I traced with my tongue yesterday. "I appreciate the ride, but I'm done now."

Maura's brows wing up. "We're still hours out from making port. You're not done quite yet."

Fool that I am, I wait for some indication that what happened between us changed anything for her. It doesn't come. Of course it doesn't. She's been consistent since the moment she pulled me from the depths.

She doesn't want me.

Not in any kind of permanent way. The future we painted together, when we were barely more than children and filled with the false assurance of our immortality, was never more than a dream. Wishing on stars as if that's ever been enough to change someone's fate.

Later, I'll mourn that future we'll never have. There's no time right now.

"I think you'll find that I am, in fact, quite done." I don't let myself pause again. One soft word from her, and I'll let doubt creep in, dissuading me from my course. I allow myself until the count of ten to study her features, make a memory to tuck close to my heart in the years to come. "Goodbye, Maura."

I make it down the stairs to the main deck before she's at my back. "Juliette, what are you doing?"

"Leaving."

"We're still leagues offshore. A selkie or one of my crew with a specialty in water might be able to swim it, but you're a magicless human. You'll drown."

I cut around the elemental users filling the sails. "Your faith in me is truly astounding."

"Don't say it like that." The exasperation in her tone is so purely Maura that I almost stop, almost turn back.

It's a lie. She's not mine. Maybe she never was.

I reach the railing and consider how best to do this. I heard the Cŵn Annwn, an old man with more nose hair than what covered his balding skull, drunkenly speak to the pretty courtier he was set on seducing.

A leap of faith, my pretty. That's the crux of it. It's not like portals or crossroads, where anyone with a bit of knowledge and poor luck can find and use them. You have to hold this piece of eight—yes, isn't it unassuming—and take a leap of faith. If you're worthy of that godsforsaken city, it will allow you entry.

Atlantis.

A city—an island—out of time and space. A crossroads to all the realms in existence, one anyone can access if they have the key and the faith that they're worthy. I don't know what makes a person worthy, but I have enough faith to take the leap. I don't have another choice.

I put a foot up on the rail.

"Juliette!" Maura grabs for my arm. "I know you're angry, but there's no reason to be foolish."

"I'm not being foolish." I jerk away and propel myself up on to the railing. "Goodbye, Maura. I hope you find everything you've ever wanted." I tighten my grip on the coin until my nails dig into my palm. "Goodbye."

I shove backward, holding her gaze as I fall toward the water. My stomach lodges itself in my throat, and all I see are Maura's green eyes, wide with shock, as the water closes over my head.

I sink a good distance, waiting for the magic to kick in. Not that I know what magic feels like, exactly. I have none of my own. But...nothing happens. *What the fuck?* I open my eyes and frown against the strange light overhead. Not like the dawn I just saw seconds ago.

There's no time to process fully, though. Not with my bag dragging me down. I fight against the pull, fight my way toward the surface, but it's quickly apparent that I perhaps misjudged things again.

I'm not the strongest swimmer, after all.

I...may have made a mistake.

A stream of bubbles appears as someone dives into the water and cuts their way down to me. I don't need to see Maura's furious face to recognize who it is. It's almost enough to make me want to stop fighting the weight of my bag and let it pull me down into the deep. Better to drown than to face the humiliation waiting for me at the surface.

Except I don't really believe that, do I? For better or worse, humiliation is something I'm incredibly familiar with. How can I not be, when every move I make personally insults my father? Nothing's ever proper enough, smart enough, *good* enough.

In this moment, with the weight of the water against my chest and darkness all around, I can admit I was relieved when he passed me over for the crown. Now, instead of disappointing an entire country, I'm only disappointing Maura.

She reaches me far faster than a magicless human could and wraps strong arms around my waist. That gets me moving. It's one thing for me to consider giving up, but I'll be damned before I drag Maura down with me.

We fight our way to the surface. This time, she doesn't bother with the ladder. "Get us out of here," she roars.

The water responds. Or that's what it seems like. We rise in a wave...and keep rising. Right to the railing of the deck. Maura hands me off to Cai and Daichi, who grip my upper arms and haul me over the railing. She follows, landing nimbly beside me.

I slump back against the railing. So much for my dramatic exit. I should have known it wouldn't work. That old bastard was just trying to get into the courtier's pants. Atlantis is a myth, and if it isn't, why would the Cŵn Annwn be carrying the key to accessing it? They would hate its existence on principle. They *do* hate it. It was there in the old man's voice.

I shake my head. I can't focus, not with the weight of salt water and failure weighing me down.

"Juliette." Maura crouches in front of me, and it's truly not fair how good she looks. She slicks back her wet hair—gods, the sight of her makes my heart skip a beat even though I know better. Or at least I *should* know better.

She grabs my shoulders. "What did you *do?*"

Oh. Oh wow. She's going to make me say it. My throat burns, but I have a lifetime of learning to hide what I'm truly thinking and feeling. I give her a bright smile. "Just a silly trick. Are you laughing? Because I'm laughing."

Maura curses. "Don't fuck with me." She drags me to my feet. "Where did you take us?" She spins me around and shoves me against the railing.

That's whe dance yep turn offn I finally register what my brain has been trying to tell me. The sky overhead is a bright blue far more vivid than the sky I'm used to. But that isn't the only thing that's changed.

There's an island in front of us. Rocks break the surface of the water, guiding my eye to the narrow entrance of a bay. But the rocks aren't the only thing that's changed. I register bits and pieces of ships, both familiar and unfamiliar, shattered amid the rocks...

And the flash of scales beneath the surface.

Maura jerks me back from the railing. "Mermaids!"

7

MAURA

If we survive this, fuck dropping Juliette at the nearest port and sending her on her way. The woman is a menace and must be contained. I'll drag her to a convent, lock her up, and throw away the key. At least then she'll be safe.

But she's not safe right now.

Mermaids.

We're in the wrong part of the world for mermaids. Or at least we were a minute ago. I have no idea where we are now. "Cai!"

"On it!" Ze sprints to the helm and wrenches it around, narrowly avoiding the biggest of the rocks ahead of us.

I drag Juliette to the clear corner behind Cai and push her into it. "Stay. I can't afford anyone to keep watch right now."

"But—"

"*Stay.*" I take the helm from Cai and start shouting orders. "Presta! Silas! Get those sails moving." It's going to be nearly impossible to navigate into that bay opening without sinking, and that's even without the mermaids harrying our flanks. "Cai! Get every fire user on the crew to form a perimeter."

Ze is already moving, shouting orders of zir own. It's tempting to keep an eye on zir, but ze has been doing this as long as I have. Ze knows what needs to be done.

I have to keep us above water long enough for the fire users to do their job. "Daichi!"

"Here." He appears at my side, almost as if by magic. "This is going to be a rough one."

"Get into the crow's nest and alert me to any dangers I can't see." That's the problem. The visible rocks are bad enough, but the ones just below the surface will sink an unwary ship. "Go."

"On it." He sprints to the mast and climbs it nimbly, helped along by his air power.

"I didn't know." Juliette speaks so softly, I almost miss the words over the sound of my crew calling alerts back and forth and the whoosh of fireballs striking the water, resulting in steam and the shrieks of mermaids.

If—when—we survive this, I fully intend to get an extremely detailed explanation of what magic Juliette just pulled. One moment I was cursing her for jumping ship, and then it was like the whole world simultaneously held its breath and skipped a beat. A blink, and the familiar waters were gone, replaced by this strange island.

No time to worry about that now. I have to get us to safe harbor.

"Left. Two degrees." Daichi's voice in my ear, carried by the wind. "There are other ships."

"I see them." Half a dozen in the waters around us, moving at speeds that make me shudder. Apparently they decided the mermaids are more dangerous than the rocks. I hope they're right. I make the adjustment. "As long as they don't fuck with us, ignore them."

"Will do." A pause. "Half a degree left. You're not quite there."

It's uncanny not being able to see what he's guiding us away from, but we've done this before. I trust him with my life, and more importantly, I trust him with the crew members' lives.

"When I give the call, right five degrees."

I hold my breath, my palms slippery on the helm. One of the nearby ships veers close enough for me to see its crew frantically fighting off several mermaids clinging to its sides. I shudder and follow Daichi's instructions.

Realistically, it only lasts a few minutes, but it feels like it takes hours to navigate through the rocks and into the relative calm of the bay. The mermaids don't follow us past the last rock... And neither do the ships. I twist and watch them continue north along the coast. *What the fuck?*

My hands won't stop shaking. We made it through the rocks and mermaids without casualties, but there's no denying the truth. We are not in waters I recognize.

Where did Juliette bring us? Because this is certainly her fault. We were transported the moment she hit the water, which means she did something to cause it. It's too big a coincidence to be anything else.

I guide us farther into the bay, the crew silent as we take in this strange place. Each harbor town feels a little different. They all have their own flavor, from their people to how they conduct business, to the style of the buildings.

This place is like nothing I've ever seen.

The buildings are a hodgepodge style, some familiar and some completely foreign in a way my mind shies away from. I'm used to magic; it's a part of life.

This feels different.

"What did you do?" I speak softly, barely containing my fury. "Where did you take us?"

"Funny story—"

"Juliette, I swear to the gods, if you spin me some yarn of a tale, I will chuck you right back into the sea, and this time I'll leave you there. What. Did. You. Do?"

"It was only supposed to be me," she mutters. She stares at the deck, not meeting my gaze. "I didn't realize it would haul you in after me, or I wouldn't have done it." She makes a face. "Though if I'd done it off the other ship, I'd be in even worse trouble, so I guess I should be grateful."

"Are you not answering my questions on purpose?" I keep my grip on the helm because I may strangle her if I let go. She's always had a tendency to ramble when she's nervous, but this is deadly serious, and I need to know what we're walking into.

At least the ships kept sailing. I don't understand why, not when there was nothing but more rocks and mermaids in front of them, but it means we aren't fighting for position at the docks.

Juliette sighs, a nearly soundless exhale. "We're in Atlantis."

Shock steals my breath. Surely she didn't just say what I think she said. "Please tell me you're joking."

"Atlantis. It's real, and it's right there." She jerks her chin at the approaching dock. "I know we always thought it was a myth, but we thought the Cŵn Annwn were a myth, too, and there's one in my father's court right now."

Too much, too fast.

Atlantis.

In all my years of sailing, I've only ever heard whispers and old fishwives' tales. As time passed, I tucked it into the same locked box that contains my soured dreams of a future with a certain princess.

Never to be.

Except the princess is standing before me, fighting between wilting and crowing with glee, and Atlantis is right fucking there.

Then the rest of what she said catches up with me. The

Cŵn Annwn. The hunters between realms. I thought they were a myth when I was sixteen, but I've learned a lot since then.

You see things at sea. Hear things. Whispers of other realms, of ships blown off course by storms that are hardly natural. Sometimes they're never seen again. Sometimes they come back, telling tales of strange sights...and ships with crimson sails.

The Cŵn Annwn are dangerous enough to make pirates who balk at nothing cross themselves against evil. If they board your ship, you're presented with a choice: join them or die. If you join them, you can never go home again.

"Tell me you didn't," I repeat. The coincidence is too large to ignore. If one of the Cŵn Annwn is at her father's court, she stole something off them that allowed her access to Atlantis. It's the only thing that makes sense.

"You're going to have to be more specific."

Her dodge may as well be a confession. I open my mouth to yell at her for being reckless, but Daichi chooses that moment to interrupt, his voice a whisper in my ear. "You have an audience, Captain."

I snap my mouth shut. Right. The crew. I will have to deal with Juliette later. Right now, I need to see us through.

"Cai."

Ze appears at my shoulder. "Yes, Captain."

"You're in charge. I'm taking a small group ashore to get the lay of the land."

Ze raises zir brows. "Are we going to talk about the mermaids?"

We aren't going to talk about any of this, at least until I know we're not going to be facing down the Cŵn Annwn...or something even worse. "Not yet. Keep the crew content, and we'll give word if it's safe."

"We're pirates. *Safe* isn't in the job description."

I give zir the look that statement deserves. I know Cai

doesn't want to be left behind, but one of us has to be here, and it won't be me. Not this time.

"I'm coming, too."

I don't look at Juliette. "Absolutely not."

"Either I go with you, or I go on my own."

I release the helm so fast, Cai has to step in and catch it before it spins. "You're out of your damn mind if you think you're leaving this ship." I advance on her, and a deep, dark part of me is delighted that she holds her ground. Juliette never knows when to bend. It probably comes from being born rich and privileged and never having to worry that someone will lay a hand on her precious royal skin.

Or maybe she knows I would cut off my hand before I raised it to her, even if I *do* want to throttle her right now. I refuse to examine how warm that makes my chest.

I lean down until my lips brush the shell of her ear. "I will truss you up and leave you in my cabin before I allow you to put yourself and my people in danger."

"I'm excellent at undoing knots and picking locks. You can't hold me."

"Watch me."

"Captain."

I bite down a curse and turn back to Cai. "What?"

"Unless you want to put a guard on her, it may be wise to take her with you." Ze's glance at Juliette isn't exactly kind. "She's the reason we're here. I don't want her pulling some more strange magic and sucking the ship in again. We run the risk of leaving you behind and being unable to return."

"I would never—"

Cai's right. She could take my ship and crew and leave me stranded. The thought leaves me sick to my stomach. What a fucking mess. If I leave her behind, she'll try to follow anyway. She may even do something foolish like attempt to swim.

The thought makes my stomach drop. "You're coming, but if

you make one wrong move, I'm gagging you and tying you to the mast."

"Yes, Captain," Juliette says meekly, every line of her pretty face repentant and innocent.

It's a lie.

Which makes me wonder what else she's lying about.

8

JULIETTE

I can't stop looking around me. It's hard to get a good gauge of the island, but it seems smaller than I imagined. Surely the fabled Atlantis should be larger than life.

This place is...almost mundane.

Not that Maura acts like it as her crew lowers a boat into the water and she directs me to follow Daichi down the rope ladder to it.

He's an attractive fellow, tall, with short black hair, broad shoulders, and light brown skin. His eyes are almost inky, and there's mischief in them as I step down next to him and take the seat he indicates.

He grins. "You've got our captain in a tizzy."

A tizzy. Maura has never been in a tizzy in her life; she doesn't know the meaning of the word. She snarls and snaps and curses, but she doesn't throw childlike tantrums.

That's my department.

Not that I do it often now. I'm an adult, after all. But my father hates what he terms *hysterics*, so indulging in that sort of thing is a surefire way to get out of difficult conversations with him. It's a moot point now.

I have absolutely no intention of going home. Ever.

Another crew member whose name I haven't caught descends the ladder, and Maura drops lightly into the boat a few seconds later. She glares at the docks. "No chance of getting in there without someone seeing us. Play this straight."

"Yes, Captain." Daichi isn't acting quick with his words now. Maura's tension has bled into our small group, and even I catch myself hunching my shoulders. It takes effort to straighten my spine and lift my chin.

I can feel Maura's gaze on me, but I ignore her. This is still goodbye, no matter what else happens. I'm sure there's a way back for *The Kelpie*; we just have to find the right person to ask.

And me?

I'm going to see what the rest of the realms have to offer. Without the future I dreamed about with Maura, there's nothing left for me in my realm. No kingdom. No throne. No lover. I only have the money in my bag, but I'll find a way forward. Anything is better than marrying some stranger and moving to a court where everyone will act the part of an enemy.

There's the small problem of the Cŵn Annwn, but surely they're not as fearsome as Maura acts. The old man visiting my father's court certainly isn't. He seemed more intent on wine and wenches than anything else. I'm still not sure why he was in court, though. To the best of my understanding, the Cŵn Annwn are essentially pirates who hunt the space between realms. They're not supposed to care about what happens in the realms themselves, only that people don't muck about in the in-between.

Personally, I have no intention of spending any time in that in-between. Which means I should be in the clear. There is the small matter of my stealing from them, but surely that old man will think he misplaced it and not realize who took it. It should be fine. Probably. Hopefully.

I'm one woman. I may not have a lot of life experience

outside my father's castle, but I'm a quick learner. I'll figure it out.

I just have to lose my angry ex first.

We barely reach the docks when I spring into action. I step off the boat, fully intending to make a smooth exit. Unfortunately, my legs haven't gotten the memo.

I read about sea legs and mentally prepared for the sway and tilt of a ship. But I didn't expect to feel like the land is moving strangely beneath my feet.

A strong hand catches my elbow, keeping me on my feet when I stumble. I look up to find Maura standing too close. Her gaze drops to my mouth and then rises to my eyes. "If you don't slow down, I swear to the gods, I will tie you up and leave you in my cabin." She tightens her grip on my elbow. "Do *not* talk to me about how good you are at slipping knots. You can't untie shit if I bind your wrists to your ankles."

"You keep threatening to tie me up." My breath catches on something in my chest. "Sounds like fun."

"Like fun," she repeats and then curses. "You are going to get yourself killed. You don't have a lick of sense."

I'll lick your sense.

I manage to keep the nonsense statement internal. Barely.

Distantly, there's a cry of a crowd. I can't tell if it's joy or rage. Crowds are tricky like that; their mood can turn dangerous without warning. I can't see it, which isn't the comfort it should be. This island isn't big enough to hide effectively if it comes to that, and even if we could get back to the ship, there are the mermaids to contend with.

Mermaids.

I've heard stories, of course, but I pictured creatures that were more majestic and less murderous. The elemental fire users were the only reason we didn't lose anyone during that harrowing experience. One we'll have to repeat to leave the island. The realization makes my stomach hurt.

Maura motions to Daichi, and he checks the rope he tossed around one of the metal ties on the dock. He frowns. "Dockmaster or someone else should be here."

"Yes." She narrows her eyes. "Let's head into town and find someone to clue us in."

Daichi grins as if she's given him a great gift. "You know where we're headed."

Maura rolls her eyes, a small smile tugging at her lips. "Of course. Gods forbid I doubt your selfish intentions."

"Never selfish. What I do, I do for my crew." He bounds off the boat and heads down the dock with long, ground-eating strides.

Maura motions at the other crew member. "Go with him, and keep him on task. We need that information more than Daichi needs his cock sucked."

"You know how he is."

"I do, but we haven't been at sea that long. He'll survive a few hours."

"Yes, Captain." They sigh and head after the navigator.

Leaving me and Maura alone.

I catch her looking at me strangely and fold my hands primly before me. "Are we going to stand here and wait?"

For a second, I think she might try to make me do exactly that. Instead, she shakes her head. "No, we're sitting ducks here. Come on."

I ignore her outstretched hand and start down the dock. The colorful buildings grouped just off the beach call to me. I didn't come all this way to play it safe. I want to explore. There are so many new experiences here, I can practically taste them.

Yes, it's a little scary, but what new experiences aren't a little scary?

We barely make it off the dock when two people dressed in black appear, almost as if by magic.

I stop short, taking them in. Both short, one lean and one

with a body type closer to mine. The lean one has dark-brown skin and bright pink hair that curls in ringlets down to their shoulders. The plump one is violet from their smooth skin to their short hair, the latter one shade darker.

The lilac one steps forward. "First time?" They grin. "Look, Brynn. Fresh meat." They lower their voice conspiratorially. "She loves fresh meat."

Brynn sighs. "I know it's their first time, River. They have the stink of shock all over them." She points to her companion. "Don't mind xyr. River likes to scare the babies."

Maura doesn't look fazed. "We don't want trouble."

"They all say that." River grins, revealing teeth that are a little too sharp to be human. All at once, I realize what xe must be. Fae. We don't have any in Skoiya. My father can't stand any authority but his, so he had those native to our lands exiled. Any found are escorted to the borders and turned out into neighboring kingdoms. Foreign Fae dignitaries won't visit our court as a result, but my father doesn't seem to care about the implications of *that*.

Brynn's hand falls to the short sword at her waist. "Any sirens among your crew?"

Maura shakes her head slowly. "No. Sirens are extinct in our realm."

"Lucky you." River still has that unsettling grin on xyr face. "But just in case you're lying and trying to be clever, know that sirens are outlawed on Atlantis. That damned aphrodisiac magic is a nightmare to deal with."

I thought sirens sang sailors to their deaths. Aphrodisiac magic sounds like fun. "We don't have sirens on the crew." I don't know why I'm speaking up. It isn't *my* crew.

Maura sends me an unreadable look but doesn't comment on my overreach. "We're looking—"

"Everyone comes here looking for something," Brynn cuts

in. "That's not our problem. You're new, which means you need to meet the monarch."

"Hope they like you. It's off to the dungeon if they don't."

I exchange a glance with Maura. Of course Atlantis would have a ruler, but this seems highly strange. Then again, what do I know of pirate politics and magical islands? My father hardly requires every sailor coming to port to announce themself personally, but foreign dignitaries certainly jump through exactly those hoops.

"Of course," Maura says smoothly. "Lead the way."

It's only as they march us away from the docks and past a truly impressive set of stocks and the fascinating buildings surrounding the square that I wonder how Daichi and the other crew member got past them.

The buildings themselves are constructed in the way of buildings everywhere—four-ish walls and a roof—but what really sets them apart from my experience is their bright colors. Green, red, every shade of blue. It's chaotic and lovely and my whole heart itches to get exploring.

There's a delightfully worn blue building beside the road heading north, its doors thrown open and music and laughter coming from within. A pretty painted sign hangs above the doorway. "The Bawdy Banquet," I read aloud. What could... Oh. *Oh.* "I am definitely going there as soon as we're done with the monarch."

Maura actually misses a step. "You are most definitely *not* going there. That's a brothel."

"Is it?" I ask sweetly. "I had no idea. I'm a virgin, you see. I don't even know what sex is."

A delightful blush colors her cheeks, and she curses. "You're a pain in the ass."

"You liked it well enough a few hours ago."

River laughs, a strange noise that almost sounds like it

echoes despite the trees pressing in on either side of the road. "I like these two, Brynn."

"Yes, well, you would. You got to eat the last person who pissed off the monarch." Brynn flicks a hand over her shoulder, urging us to pick up our pace. "A little courtesy information since you obviously don't know much about this place."

"Which begs the question of how you got here in the first place," River murmurs.

Brynn ignores xyr. "We don't have many laws here, but those we do are upheld by the monarch. All pay fealty to them. They're fair enough, but if you cross them, the consequences aren't pretty."

"How do we leave the island?" Maura asks it so casually, as if it's not the thing she wants most in the world.

"A few ways out." Brynn shrugs. "There are portals scattered in these trees, but I don't recommend utilizing them."

I glance curiously at the trees. Like the buildings in the square, they're a fascinating mix of familiar and fantastical. The combination both draws me and repulses me. I might not have spent much time in nature, but even I know that bright colors often function as a warning. Which means the twisting tree with vivid orange mushrooms growing out of it is nothing but trouble. I decide right then and there that the portals in the woods are a last resort only. It would be better to hop on some other ship.

"And the others?"

"Start sailing and hope for the best." River pats xyr hair, making xyr curls bounce. "Or I guess you could play it safe and buy a spell from the old witch in the square."

Maura lifts her brows. "You have to buy a spell every time you leave?"

"Regulars are granted permanent spells by the monarch." Brynn lifts her head. "Ah, we're here."

9

MAURA

This situation only gets more fucked the longer we're here. I need to be focusing on getting my ship and my crew out of this realm and back to ours, but I'm achingly aware of the wide-eyed way Juliette stares at everything. The first time I turn around, she's going to be in those woods and falling into a portal.

I should be saying good riddance. I came for her when she called for help, but I didn't agree to jump realms and put everyone under my care in danger. Maybe I should have left her to the fate of her foolishness...

No.

We may not have a future, and I may be a coldhearted bitch of a pirate, but even I don't have it in me to stand back and let her be harmed. Which means I need to figure out how to get her back on my ship and home.

But first we have to meet this mystery monarch and not get ourselves murdered in the process. I've dealt with plenty of people who fashion themselves leaders of port towns, so I know enough to keep my mouth shut until I get a proper read on the situation.

Juliette...does not.

I catch her elbow as we climb the hill to the impressive stone structure that would do any lordling proud. "Let me do the talking."

"Oh, do you have a lot of experience with convincing royalty not to call for your head?" She smiles so sweetly, I almost miss the fact it doesn't reach her eyes. Juliette is *furious* with me. I don't know why the realization startles me, but it does.

"I am trying to keep you alive," I snarl.

"I've been doing just fine on my own for twenty-six years. I didn't ask for you to babysit me."

"Living a pampered life as a princess is not the same thing, and you know it." I force myself to keep my grip on her light even as I want to drag her down the hill and toss her back on the boat. "And you *did* ask for me to babysit you when you called for help."

"You've helped me. It's done. You're free to go."

"Ladies." Brynn puts a stop to our bickering with a single word. She motions at the dark door in front of us. "Follow the hallway. It will lead you to the monarch."

I pause. "You're not going to escort us?"

"Follow the golden path." River laughs that uncanny laugh. "If you stray, no one can be held accountable for where you end up."

I make a face. "More portals?"

"This is Atlantis." Xe turns and flicks xyr hair off xyr shoulders. "See you around. If you live."

Brynn drags a hand over her face. "Look, xe is right about one thing. Stay on the golden path. It will lead you in and lead you out. You're safe enough if you follow instructions."

Safe enough isn't exactly safe, but it's too late to change our minds. Juliette has already moved to wrestle the large door open. If I stand around arguing, she's liable to do exactly the opposite of what's instructed. She's always been as curious as a cat, and nowhere near as lucky. "Slow down, Juliette."

She ignores me, because of course she does. I mutter under my breath, Brynn's chuckle following me through the door and into the dark hallway lit by sconces. On the stone floor beneath our feet, there's a single line of gold leading deeper into the shadows.

Juliette whistles softly. "This monarch has a flair for the dramatic. I like it."

I follow one step behind her, eyeing the dark doorways as we pass them. Sounds come from several—laughter and moaning and whispers that practically invite one to lean in and listen. "It's a trap."

"Of course it's a trap." I can't see Juliette roll her eyes, but the sensation is there in her tone. "Everything about this place is a trap. It wouldn't have survived this long if that weren't true."

She's not wrong. I'm not entirely how it exists in the first place, not when the Cŵn Annwn are so notorious for hunting down anyone who wanders in between realms. As best I can understand, Atlantis exists outside of realms, which means it should be under their domain. At least in theory. That obviously isn't the case, but I don't know enough about either faction to know *why*.

I suppose the details don't matter. It all adds up to danger. We're in over our heads.

I take two quick steps to catch up with Juliette. "We'll talk to the monarch, and then we'll head back to the square and get the exit spell in place."

"No."

Fuck, but I knew it wouldn't be that easy. "What do you mean no?"

"It's a very simple word. Only two letters. I know you're familiar with it."

"I understand what 'no' means," I grit out. "I'm asking you

why the fuck you're telling me no now, when I am only trying to keep you safe."

Juliette peers down a particularly dark hallway where someone giggles in a way that makes the hair on my arms stand on end. She makes no move to approach it. "You're not trying to keep me safe, Maura. You're trying to dump me in the nearest port and move on with your life, your conscience unblemished."

I snort. "You know my reputation. My conscience has plenty marring it."

"Not when it comes to me." She says it softly, but the words don't waver. "Not until now. It's different. No matter what else is true between us, don't pretend like it's the same." She moves forward before I can come up with a response.

It's just as well. I have no response. Juliette isn't wrong. I may target the rich and corrupt; I may steal, murder, and occasionally indulge in some flat-out mayhem, but she's always been a soft spot in my history. A moment when maybe things could have been different, a branch in the path of my life. It's a naive thought, but that almost makes it more special as a result.

The hallway ends abruptly. One moment we're hurrying past what feel like infinite doorways, and the next, we're standing at the edge of a large room. The windows overlooking the sea to the north make it feel even more spacious, as if that were possible. I catch a glimpse of something red on the horizon, but there's no time to focus on it.

The monarch is easy enough to pick out. They lounge on something that could be considered a throne, one leg casually tossed over the arm of the chair. They're wearing black just like the rest of the court around them, billowing pants that gather at their ankles and a corset inlaid with what appear to be black jewels. I lift my gaze to their face and pause. They're absolutely stunning. Medium-brown skin that's almost unnaturally smooth, short curly black hair, horns that curve gracefully back over their head, and dark eyes that take us in.

I start forward, but Juliette beats me there. I'm still wondering *how* she moved so quickly when she drops into a low curtsy. Gone is the stubborn chaos monster, replaced by a pretty princess. It doesn't matter that her dress has seen better days and her hair is slightly stiff from salt water. She manages to make it look intentional. It's not magic, but it might as well be.

"Your Majesty."

The monarch's lips curve a little, and they flick their fingers at Juliette. "Rise. We don't do that here."

"I always prefer to err on the side of formality." She beams at them. "You have a lovely island."

They raise their eyebrows, that small smile that could mean anything still in place. "It's been quite some time since we've hosted actual royalty. What brings you here, Princess?"

How could they possibly know? We've been on the island only an hour or so, and neither Juliette nor I really talked about her position since docking. It can't be spies, so it must be magic. A seer?

While I eye the people gathered around the monarch, Juliette speaks. "I've heard of Atlantis's reputation, and I wanted to see for myself." She pauses, and it's the only warning I get before she throws all my plans to see her safely home out the window. "And my realm holds nothing for me any longer. I seek another."

The monarch's dark gaze flicks to me. Shock has stolen my ability to shield my expression, and there's no way they miss it. They drop their foot to the ground and lean forward. "Your friend here seems unhappy with that decision."

"I am my own person."

"So I see." They give another of those brief smiles. "Enjoy

all the hospitality Atlantis has to offer, Princess. When you're ready to leave, return here, and we'll see you somewhere safe."

My jaw drops. "Wait, no."

They look at me again. "Do you challenge our decree, Captain?"

Juliette sinks into another deep curtsy. "Of course not, Your Majesty. Thank you so much for your hospitality. I will enjoy it to the fullest."

"I imagine you will." Their tone isn't warm, exactly, but there's an indulgent thread there that makes me want to snarl. It takes two beats for the thorny sensation in my stomach to register. *Jealousy.* This monarch is looking at Juliette with hungry eyes, and I want to step between them and reach for my sword.

It's not smart nor savvy, not an action that will do anything but put myself and my crew in danger. Even knowing that, I have to plant my feet to keep from doing it.

The monarch, damn them, sees my reaction. They study me for a long moment, but when they speak, it's for Juliette. "If you would like to enjoy my...personal hospitality...come back and see me without your overprotective captain in tow. We would enjoy each other."

"You honor me," Juliette murmurs as she rises from her curtsy. I'm not sure how she manages it, but she slams her foot down on mine without missing a beat. "I will absolutely consider it."

"Good." They wave a graceful hand. "You're dismissed. The way back will be easier."

This time, Juliette is the one to grab my arm and all but drag me out of the room. She doesn't speak until we're outside the castle, charging down the road far too quickly. "Well, that was brilliant. You were going to threaten the *monarch* who rules this entire island. What were you thinking?"

"I wasn't going to threaten them." I almost sound like I mean it.

She glares. "Don't lie to me. You had the same look on your face right before you punched Bradley Lee in the face when he tried to get me to flash my tits."

The memory of that shit-for-brains fool makes me clench my fists all over again. "He was going to yank down your dress. I stopped him."

"You broke his nose, and then you managed to dislocate his jaw. He *still* almost pisses himself every time he sees me."

"He should be grateful for the broken nose, because if he managed to assault the crown princess, he would have been hanged." That thorny feeling inside me twists and twines through my guts. "You still see him. Why? He's the baker's son."

"They make the best bread in Ashye. I'm careful. He doesn't know who I am. No one in the main city does when I wear my disguise." Juliette throws up her hands and curses. "This is exactly what I'm talking about. You were going to draw your sword and attack the most powerful person on this dangerous magical island."

She's not entirely wrong, but the shame her words bring only fuels my frustration and anger. "We wouldn't *be* on this dangerous magical island if it weren't for your recklessness."

"Yes, we've covered this." She rolls her eyes. "And after you planned on returning me to my father, were you just going to shed a single tear when I was assassinated in my new spouse's court? Or were you planning on fighting the entirety of Edrines, too?"

That stops me short. "What are you talking about?" *Spouse? Assassination attempts?*

"You know everything. Surely you know about my engagement. And you're not a fool, so it's only common logic that my new stepchildren will want me dead before I can become pregnant with another competitor for the throne." When I just stare in shock, some of her anger dims. "Well, it's a moot point now. I appreciate you coming for me, and also that outstanding goodbye sex, but you've made it clear you want nothing to do with me, and *I've* made it clear I have no intention of returning to our realm. Our time together is done. Go secure the spell to leave, and I'll make my own way."

She's speaking logic, but I hate it. "I'm not leaving you here."

"I am an adult, same as you. If you try to take me back to your ship, I will not go willingly. I imagine the monarch will have some thoughts on *that*." Juliette turns and walks away.

She's right. I know she's right. But if I do as she says and secure the spell to exit Atlantis, leaving her behind to jump realms...I'll never see her again.

That shouldn't be reason enough to fight her, not when I had every intention of putting her on a carriage back to Ashye and her pampered life as Skoiya's princess. But at least then, I'd know she was out there somewhere, that perhaps one day I would hunt a royal ship with special cargo, that we'd see each other again if it was meant to be.

If I leave her here, this truly is the end for us. It's what I'm supposed to want, but the very idea is repellant right down to the very fiber of my being.

I can't do it.

I won't.

10

JULIETTE

I can hear Maura stomping behind me as I descend the road toward the town, but I don't look back, and I don't slow down. I am so damned tired of her hypocrisy. She doesn't want me, but she doesn't want anyone else to have me, either. She certainly doesn't care that if I return to my father's court, I'm destined for a life of misery in the north.

Well, I will not go quietly.

There are significantly more people around than there were when we passed through before. This must be the crowd we heard when we arrived. Some are chatting excitedly about a ship race, while others are bemoaning lost bets. Many of them seem to have started in The Bawdy Banquet and then poured out into the square.

I head for the brothel. I'm half listening to Maura behind me, so I manage to deftly step aside when she tries to grab my arm. She curses, and I give her a sweet look. "Do you always manhandle your lovers?"

"You're not— This isn't—"

Why do I have to keep poking her? It's not going to give me the response I want. She couldn't have made it clearer she wants nothing more to do with me, and yes, we had sex in her cabin, but it was goodbye sex. There's a fractured sensation in my chest that will bring me to my knees as soon as I allow myself to feel it, but for now, this place is rife with distractions.

"Juliette." There's something dangerous in Maura's voice. "If you go into that brothel, I will not be held accountable for my actions."

"Are you listening to yourself?" I toss up my hands. "You don't want me."

"What gave you that idea?" Then she's there in front of me, catching my hips and pulling me close. The feeling of her hands on me, even in this brief contact, makes me shake. I *hate* that it makes me shake. I hate even more the way her gaze catches and lingers on my lips as if she's thinking about tasting me. "I've always wanted you," she says roughly.

Liar.

I don't say it. We've hurt each other enough to last a lifetime, even if the only villain is time spent apart and a world that says a princess and a pirate can never be together.

Fuck time and fuck the world.

I may be able to say that, but I'm only one half of the equation. Maura seems to have taken that rule to heart. I lick my lips, shivering when she follows the movement. "This only ends in pain. Let me go. If you don't, I'll end up hating you, and I don't think I can bear it."

Maura blinks and tightens her grip on my hips. "I'm trying to do right by you. That's all I've ever wanted to do."

That's the problem. I don't want a savior worthy of me or other such nonsense. I want *her*. It doesn't matter how I say it or how we argue. She refuses to believe it.

Either that, or...

Or maybe it was never real for her, not in the same way it was real for me. Maybe I was the only one believing that wishes on stars could come true as I planned out a future where we were together and no one could keep us apart. Maybe I'm the sole fool who clung to that future even as the world tried to prove it for a lie.

She is one of the fiercest people I know. How can she be anything else when she's effectively dodged the royal navy and created a fearsome reputation for herself in under ten years? If she really wanted to be with me, she would have found a way.

One failure wouldn't have been enough for her to sail away and never return.

"You would have found a way," I repeat aloud. "If you really wanted me, if it ever meant anything to you, you would have found a way for us to be together."

Maura doesn't answer, and it's just as well. There's nothing to say to make this right. Not anymore. We've both come too far.

I walk into The Bawdy Banquet with my head held high. Small round tables populate the main floor, most of them filled with people of every shape, size, and paranormal flavor. I even catch sight of a demon in the back corner, horns curving from their eye sockets and temples.

It's a feast for the senses, and I fully intend to take advantage.

"Looking for something particular, my dear?"

I glance at the old woman leaning against the bar. She's wearing a gown that seems too luxurious for this place, but who am I to judge? The years mark her pale skin with deep wrinkles, but there's something timeless about her that suggests she's not what she seems.

"I don't know," I answer honestly. "It's all a little over-whelming."

Her eyes light up. "Fresh meat." She grins. "I have just the thing for you." Before I can respond, she snaps her fingers. "Nadia."

A woman appears at her shoulder, a redhead so beautiful,

she takes my breath away. Her skin is the kind of porcelain color that suggests it's never felt the touch of the sun, and she's busty in a way that would normally make my mouth water.

The old woman raises her brows. "Not to your taste? I have many people who work for me. Tell me what you like, and I'll provide."

I don't know what it is about this stranger that prompts honesty from me again, but when I open my mouth, the truth emerges. "Normally, I would take you up on it, but I'm..." What? Not in a relationship. Not exclusive. Not *anything*. "It's complicated."

"Mmm. Complicated." She says the word as if tasting its flavor. "Is it the kind of complicated that's tall, blonde, and furious?"

I tense. The temptation to look over my shoulder is almost overwhelming, but I somehow manage to resist. "She's sending a lot of mixed messages."

The old woman waggles her eyebrows. "The best way to get over an old lover is to get under a new one." She nudges Nadia with her shoulder. "Get the lady a drink, Nadia. Let her pour out her woes."

I most certainly will not be doing *that* to a stranger. Not when I know how brothels work when it comes to information. People say the damnedest things when they're out of their mind with pleasure and enjoying the aftermath of a good orgasm. I've used it to my benefit a time or twelve. My father might not take me seriously, but several of his advisors have been happy with the information I've passed along from using that method with foreign dignitaries.

I'm not about to fall into that trap here.

But the only other option is to turn around and leave, and I won't do that. Not when I can feel Maura glaring at me. "A drink sounds lovely."

Nadia smiles with practiced ease and slips her arm into mine. "This way, love."

I swear, I feel Maura follow us deeper into the room. Nadia leads me to a small table tucked back into an alcove. It's not truly isolated, but it dampens the noise of the place and feels private. Somewhere close to the front, music starts, a slow sensual tune that makes my skin prickle. Or maybe that's the fury of my ex bearing down on us.

"She's very beautiful," Nadia murmurs.

"Yes, she is." I almost sit in the chair that would put my back to the room, but even I'm not coward enough to do that. Instead I perch on the seat next to Nadia. "You really don't have to entertain me. This is likely going to devolve into a fight."

She smiles sweetly. "This is The Bawdy Banquet, love. There are fights every hour on the hour, and usually for less reason. It's part of our charm."

Maura is having a hard time making her way through the tables toward us. I'm not certain if it's intentional on the part of the people gathered or coincidence, but she has to stop every other step and maneuver around a drunk sailor or a giggling sex worker or, in one laughable case, a parrot that descends from *somewhere* to flap in her face.

I sigh. "She's furious."

"She'll be a few minutes." Nadia leans closer, her shoulder soft against mine. "Eloise was right, you know. Sometimes the best way to deal with a possessive ex is to...provoke...them."

I give her a look. "Maura isn't possessive." Jealous in the way a child can be when someone picks up a toy they discarded, but possessiveness indicates a desire for keeping. Maura doesn't feel that for me. She's more than proven that at this point.

Nadia laughs, a musical sound that makes me lean closer despite myself. "You learn the look of possessiveness in my line of work. Your captain is rife with it." She smiles slowly. "I'll prove it to you. Lean closer."

I obey without thinking, shifting until our faces are kissably close. Nadia cups my face with one hand, her mischievous smile still in place. "Don't look now, but I think she may start flipping tables to get to us. A kiss may push her right over the edge."

It seems to defy belief that she's right, but I can hear Maura cursing halfway across the room. Shock steals through me. "She really *is* possessive."

"Told you so." Nadia strokes my cheek with her thumb. "Jealousy and possession can be a lovely spice if you're in the mood for something more intimate."

I almost take her up on it. I'm hurting and confused, and it feels like every time I turn around, Maura is there, adding to that confusion. She supposedly wants me safe, but she'll happily send me back to my gilded cage in my father's castle, and then beyond it to Edrines where I'll be in active danger.

Still...it feels wrong to flaunt Nadia in front of her, no matter how beguiling the woman is. "I can't do that to her."

"You're doing it to her right now." But Nadia drops her hand, still smiling. "You really do love her, don't you?"

It's such a bold thing to say that I almost deny it on instinct. The words still in my throat. It's the truth. I love Maura. I have since I was a kid. Her not wanting me doesn't change that.

I expect Maura to appear in a rage, but when I finally look, she's standing next to Eloise with her head bowed to be even with the older woman's. What's that about? I turn back to Nadia. "You seem nice."

She bursts out laughing. "Honey, if you're about to let me down gently, rest assured that it's not necessary. You're cute, but I'll live."

There's no reason for my pride to get stung over that. I'm the one doing the rejecting. Then again, it just feels like I'm utterly replaceable.

"You."

I blink up to find Maura standing over our table, an unreadable expression on her face. She jerks her thumb at Nadia. "Get lost."

Nadia hesitates two full beats. When she rises, it's as if she chose to do it rather than followed Maura's command. It's a neat trick. I watch her walk away from us, a sway in her hips, for longer than I should. Maybe I'm a coward. I don't want to look at Maura, don't want to have the same conversation *again*. I don't know how many times and different ways she can tell me she doesn't want me.

"Come on." She holds out her hand.

I find myself reaching for it and jerk my hand back. "No."

"Juliette." She sinks a thread of heat into my name that has me clenching my thighs together. "I am sweaty and sticky and in desperate need of a bath. Daichi won't be finished for another hour or so. You can sit here and pout, or you can come up to the room I just rented and bathe. It's your choice."

"Now you're just playing dirty."

"Yep." She grins, quick and fierce. Her smile makes my stomach flip, and I slip my hand into hers without having any intention of doing it. She squeezes my hand and pulls me to my feet. "Let's get you clean."

11

MAURA

Seeing Juliette with another woman made several things clear to me all at the same time. No matter what else is true, I hate seeing Juliette with other people. She might not be meant for me, but she feels like mine. She always will.

I tried to do the right thing; I tried to put her on a carriage back home where she's meant to be a pampered princess whose every desire is seen to. I *tried*. If she's so determined to abandon her life, to the point that she'll leave our entire realm behind...leave *me* behind...

She was never going to go home.

The realization sweeps over me, as dangerous as a hurricane. The only thing keeping me from making her mine forever was that last shred of nobility inside me that no one else ever acknowledged...except Juliette. To the point where it felt like that nobility was hers, and hers alone.

Except she doesn't want my nobility. Maybe she never did.

As I lead her up the stairs, her palm warm against mine, my selfishness takes over. If I give Juliette half a chance, she'll be hopping into the first portal she finds without a second thought. She's so determined to move forward that she's not thinking about the potential consequences. And right now, she sees me as something adjacent to an enemy, someone who is standing in her way.

She won't believe me if I tell her I've changed my mind, and rightfully so. There's nothing stopping me from lying to her. I could whisper exactly what she wants to hear into the pretty curve of her ear, and then when we return to our realm, I could resume my original plan to see her home.

I have no intention of doing so, but she doesn't know that.

I'll just have to show her.

The room the witch directed me to use is much nicer than I expected. It's bright and airy, courtesy of the round windows stationed high on the wall. They make the space feel bigger, while also offering plenty of privacy. The walls are painted a rich teal that brings to mind some of the southern seas that I enjoy sailing. Places where the wind is balmy on your skin and the sea is as warm as bathwater.

I would like to take Juliette there someday.

She pulls her hand from mine as I close the door behind me. "Well, that's one big bathtub."

I follow her gaze and raise my brows as I see that it is, in fact, a giant bathtub. I don't use the term *orgy-sized* lightly, but there's no other way to describe it. It's shaped approximately the same as other claw-footed bathtubs I've seen in the past, but it's easily wide enough for four people to stretch out comfortably. It's also filled with lightly steaming water, as promised.

A mosaic tile pattern covers the floor, a spiraling flurry of blues and greens and silver that should be overwhelming but instead adds to the calming feeling of the room. There's a drain in the center of the space, hidden just below the bathtub. I have to wonder if this room was built around the massive tub or if magic is behind its presence here. It doesn't matter; I'm here with a different aim.

If I try to coax Juliette into the water, we'll be here all day; in some cases it's simply better to lead. There's also the added bonus of giving her something to look at... Well, that's a side effect I'm more than happy to cultivate.

"What are you doing?"

"I think that is self-explanatory." I disarm myself, removing the knives tucked away in various places and carefully unbuckling my scabbard so I can lay it down. Strange how I am still fully clothed but feel naked without a bit of steel on me.

This is Juliette, though. The only danger here is to my heart.

My shirt is next. I pull it over my head and drop it next to my weapons. If I take my time pulling off my boots and working my pants down my legs, it's only because I can feel Juliette watching me. Her gaze is like a weight upon my skin, a featherlight stroke of her fingertips down my spine. Every time I think I'll get used to wanting this woman, we spend several seconds alone and I desire her all the more.

Once I am fully naked, I turn to face her.

Juliette grew up in one of the richest and most beautiful courts in our realm. People there make beauty into a weapon and an art form by turns. I know what I look like, scarred and weathered from my time as captain of *The Kelpie*. What traditional beauty I possess has been sharpened until I'd stand out in her perfumed court like a barracuda among rainbow fish.

Juliette's not looking at me like that. Her eyes are large in her face as she takes me in, shock turning to liquid heat in those big eyes. "Maura," she says slowly. "Are we bathing, or are you trying to seduce me?"

"Why not both?" My voice has a careless edge that is purely a lie. As if I don't care one way or another. As if I'm not holding my breath while her gaze travels over me. "Like you said...it's a big tub."

She presses her lips together and exhales shakily. "I'm still very angry with you."

"I know." I can't pretend I've had a single clear thought from the moment I got her distress call.

"I'm not going back to Ashye."

"I know that, too."

She keeps worrying her bottom lip until I want to reach over and soothe it with my thumb. I have to actually clench my fists to keep from reaching for her. This needs to be *her* decision. I can't wipe the slate clean—no magic exists to do that—but I can start making the right decisions now.

The decisions that result in Juliette permanently in my life.

It's amazing how good it feels to stop fighting my need for her. It's as if I spent my energy keeping myself from her, and now there's no more reason to do that. Cai will give me shit for pivoting on a dime, but I feel like I've been turning in this direction for ten damn years.

"No point in letting the water get cold."

Juliette raises her brows. "Pretty sure that water is spelled to keep warm."

It is. I can feel the magic in the water, the careful balance that keeps it the perfect temperature for bathing. I shrug. "The point stands."

We're doing it again. The thing where we talk in circles around each other when I think we both want the same thing. We're too damned prideful. It's amazing how much clearer I see things now that I'm not fighting myself.

I climb into the tub. The water is warmer than I initially thought, and I hiss out a breath as it hits my skin. It takes all of a second to get used to it, and I slip down into the groove designed for sitting with a sigh of relief. I can hear Juliette moving, but I don't look over. I just rest my head on the lip of the tub and close my eyes.

"I'm only doing this because I'm tacky from the salt water and desperately need to wash my hair."

"Mm-hmm."

"I'm serious, Maura." A rustle of fabric as her dress hits the floor. "You have been an unbelievable ass since you showed up. I realize I called for help, but that doesn't change the fact you hurt me." She stops short, as if she didn't mean to say that aloud. When she speaks again, her voice is softer, more like the teenager she used to be. "No one wants me. Not my father. Not my city. Not my kingdom. I thought you'd be the exception, and finding out that you aren't..."

Oh fuck. I can't let that stand.

I open my eyes and turn to look at her. Juliette stands a short distance from the tub, completely naked. My words dry up, faltering on my tongue. Gods, but she's beautiful. She's so devastatingly *soft*. Round breasts capped with brown nipples. Her stomach curved like the rolling hills of her homeland. Wide hips with a scattering of stretch marks that I crave tracing with my fingertips. Soft thighs dimpled in a way that catches the light. She's not perfect, but so real, it hits me that this isn't a dream. She's not going to slip through my fingers the moment I wake up...as long as I don't fuck this up.

"I want you," I finally manage. I lick my lips, trying to measure my words in a way that won't leave room for misunderstanding. In the end, they tumble from my lips, as blunt as blocks. "I never stopped wanting you. But I know what my life is like, Juliette. It's not safe and not luxurious and not one I could ever ask you to submit yourself to. You deserve the best of everything life has to offer, and I can't give you that."

"Maura." She takes a step toward the tub, then stops. "Don't you think I should be able to decide what I want for myself?"

It sounds so reasonable. It *is* reasonable. But that ignores some really vital differences in life experience. "What you know of the world—"

"I'm going to stop you there." She holds up a hand. "If you're about to tell me that I don't know enough to make this decision for myself, then I'm going to be required to put my clothes back on and storm off. Can we just have a truce? At least long enough to bathe?"

I'm doing it again, boggling this despite my best efforts. Maybe it's better if we don't talk at all. "Yes. Truce."

She eyes me warily as if she doesn't believe me, but she does finish crossing the distance between us and climbs into the tub. Juliette lets out a low moan. "This is exactly what I needed."

I watch her breasts bob gently in the water. Yes, this is what I need, too. "I would like to wash your hair."

"Maura, I don't need..." She meets my gaze. I don't know what my face is doing, but whatever it is makes her nod slowly. "I'd like that."

She shifts forward, and I slip behind her, settling her between my thighs. There's a small table next to the tub with a wide variety of bottles in different bright colors. I eye them and the labels shift, magic translating the words to a language I understand. I blink. That's some hefty magic. Translation spells aren't cheap, but normally they're tattooed onto a person rather than an object. For the witch to have this many of them casually sitting around speaks of the kind of power that makes my skin prickle.

Except...

It wasn't just the witch. The names on the buildings were readable, and the monarch spoke in a language I recognized. I shiver. There must be magic on the whole island, which is convenient but also mildly terrifying.

I shove it out of my mind and grab the shampoo bottle. It feels so damn good to work the soapy liquid into the dark strands of Juliette's wet hair. I go much slower than I need to, suddenly determined to see every inch clean. It doesn't hurt that she gives these sweet little exhales every time I massage her scalp.

"I'm still mad at you," she moans.

"I know." I guide her to rinse her hair. The shampoo is something floral that makes my head spin. It's not a conscious decision to skate my fingers over Juliette's shoulders, but her shiver makes me do it again. "Juliette—"

"No." She turns and presses her fingers to my lips. "Don't ruin it."

She kisses me before I can tell her that I have no intention of ruining it. I almost draw away, almost press to talk about the future, but then I remember how I continually fuck things up with words. Instead of pushing her away, I grab her soft waist and pull her closer.

Yes. This. This is what we need.

I will *show* her that I have no intention of sending her away.

That I want to keep her.

Forever.

12

JULIETTE

I must be a special kind of fool. It's the only explanation for my current position, naked in a tub with Maura, her mouth on mine. But no matter what else has changed between us, *this* hasn't. Her hands on me, pulling me tight to her lean body as if she wants to merge us together in a permanent way. As if she can't stand even a breath of distance between us.

As if she loves me.

I can't think about that right now. If I do, I'll go down the road to our shared past and start wondering where it all went wrong. I don't have Maura for very long. This will be the last time we collide like two shooting stars against the night-dark sky.

If I can never have her again, I want every memory I can store. It'll have to last me the rest of my days.

Maura urges me to straddle her, and the bathtub is more than big enough to make that comfortable. I have half a mind to drive this the same way I drove our encounter in her cabin, but she doesn't give me a chance.

She digs her hand into my hair right at the base of my scalp and tugs. It's not a harsh pull, but it sends a shock of pure need through me all the same. She kisses her way down my jaw to my throat, giving me just a hint of her teeth. I can't stop shaking. It's creating little tremors in the water, and maybe another time, I'd hate that outward proof of how much she affects me, but I can't think about that right now. I can't think of anything but her.

"You drive me out of my damned mind," she murmurs against my skin. I don't have an answer for that, but apparently I don't need to give one. Maura urges me up and releases my hair to cup my breasts. She makes a sound that's nearly tormented, and then her mouth is on me.

I grip the edge of the tub behind her to stay in place as she kisses and licks and nips her way over the curve of one breast and back up the other. The demon woman avoids my nipples altogether, lavishing me with pleasure that has me writhing. She presses my breasts together and, with a wicked glance at me, flicks my nipples with her tongue. It's a light touch, a teasing one.

It's nowhere near enough.

"More," I gasp. "Harder."

Her chuckle is dark with promise. She pinches one nipple even as she sucks the other into her mouth, setting her teeth carefully against me. It's perfect. Too perfect. I whimper, my hips swiveling as I seek the friction I need.

She knows. Of course she knows.

Maura shifts and presses her thigh up between my legs, directly against my pussy. "Take what you need." And then her mouth is back on my nipple, her fingers working the other in rhythmic pinching motions that send sizzling need through me.

I grind down on her thigh, doing exactly as she commanded. Taking what I need. Even as my pleasure winds around me, tighter and tighter, my orgasm remains out of reach. I sob out my frustration. "I can't get there."

Maura doesn't hesitate. She pulls some fancy move that ends with me between her thighs once more. Her breasts press to my back, and I try to turn to face her. If I can't finish, at least I can make her come.

"No." She tightens her grip on my waist. "Relax. You're rushing things."

"There's no time." It's true in every sense of the word. This bath won't last forever. Our time together won't, either. It's all going to end, and I don't know what I'll do then. For all my bravado about starting a new life, I always planned on it being *with* Maura.

Not leaving her behind permanently.

"There's time." She shifts my hair to the side and kisses the side of my neck. "We have all the time in the world, Juliette."

"But—"

"Close your eyes."

Once again, I obey without thought. I am so bloody tired of fighting. It feels like I've been doing it my entire life, even if it might not seem that way from the outside. I thought Maura understood that...and maybe she does.

She cups my breasts and then runs her hands over my stomach. "You are so beautiful," she whispers, her voice low. "You make me wild with need. You did even before I knew what to do with you." She palms my pussy. It's such a possessive move that I jolt even as liquid desire melts my bones and leaves me restless.

"I thought we weren't talking," I finally manage.

"Is this talking?" She gently works her fingers through my folds. She's being a little tease, winding me tighter but seeming to deliberately hold back that last push I require. Maura circles my entrance with one finger. "I prefer to say it's spilling truths."

"Maura, *please*."

"What do you need?" I can hear her smile. "This?" She presses her finger into me, but only to the first knuckle.

"More!"

"Greedy." She says it like it's a compliment. Like she *delights* in it. She works her finger a little deeper into me. "This isn't enough for you, is it? You need more, Jules."

Later, I worry about the fact she's calling me *Jules*. Maura is many things, but she's not usually cruel. Not to me. Not even when we're on opposite sides of an argument. Calling me *Jules*, a nickname that's only ever belonged to her, cannot be termed anything but cruel when she means to let me go.

It doesn't matter. This feels too good to stop.

"More."

She chuckles. "Apparently I'm not pleasing you. Tell me what you want. *Explicitly.* I know you can use your words. Do it now."

Use my words? I can barely think with her wrapped around me like this, her finger pulsing inside me. But it's not enough, and it won't be enough until I do as she commands. I lick my lips and drag in a rough breath. "Two fingers."

Immediately, Maura works a second finger into me. I almost exhale in relief, but she doesn't move after that. To my horror and delight, I realize she intends for me to dictate exactly what I want from her.

Maddening woman.

"Fuck me with your fingers. Slowly." I hold my breath as she obeys, sliding her fingers in and out of me with agonizing thoroughness. "Don't stop."

I can't help melting back against her. My eyes drift shut as I'm buoyed by the water, and Maura, and the pleasure she deals out. It's not enough to make me orgasm, but for once I'm not in a hurry. I'm not sure who's actually in charge of this moment. Me with my commands, or Maura for insisting on the commands in the first place.

I'm not sure it matters.

"Does it feel good, Jules?"

I clamp my lips shut, determined not to give her the satisfaction of knowing exactly how good it feels. It doesn't matter. She knows. She presses another light kiss to the spot behind my ear. Somehow, in all these years and all my lovers, no one but Maura has ever kissed me there. It feels like a secret just between us, and the sheer bittersweetness of the moment nearly draws tears to my eyes.

"It's okay. You don't have to tell me with your words. I can feel how much you're enjoying this." She keeps up that slow, thorough fucking as if we have all the time in the world. Maybe we do. The bathwater certainly isn't cooling anytime soon, and dawn is many hours away. If I stay silent, will she spend every one of those hours doing exactly this?

Part of me wants to find out.

"I've missed you." She speaks the words so softly, they can barely be qualified as a whisper. Almost as if she's talking to herself rather than to me.

My heart gives a painful lurch. Those are words I have desperately wanted to hear, but it's hard to relish them with so much pain between us. She spent days telling me she wants to see the back of me, and now she says she missed me? I have every intention of staying silent, but my hurt and need get the better of me. "I'm tired of this."

She goes still. Her body is so tense around mine that she acts the part of a cage. She does not, however, withdraw her fingers from my pussy. "If you want something to change, you only have to ask."

If I want something to change...

I might laugh if I weren't so close to crying. I've asked for what I need, and the only response I've gotten is rejection. But that's not what she's talking about, is it? This is only sex. I'm suddenly terrified that it has only ever been sex between us.

If that's the truth, then so be it.

"I'm tired of hearing you speak. I want you to put your mouth to better use." This time, I don't give her the chance to tell me to be explicit. "I want your mouth on me, Maura. I want your tongue in my pussy, fucking me until I come. I don't want to hear another godsdamned word out of you."

She's silent for several beats. Just long enough for guilt to worm through me. I'm being an asshole, and we both know it. In that moment, I can't help but wonder if maybe she's been right all along. Maybe us being in such proximity is a recipe for disaster; we can't seem to stop hurting each other, intentionally or no.

Maura eases her fingers out of me, dragging them slowly up and over my clit. She reverses the path she took initially, tracing her way up my stomach to cup my breasts, drift over my nipples, and finally dropping away. "Very well."

She nudges me forward and slips out from behind me. Once again, I am treated to the gloriousness that is Maura. Her muscles move smoothly beneath wet scarred skin. She looks good enough to devour whole, but that's not what I'm supposed to be doing tonight.

I don't know if Maura has ever obeyed anyone even once in her life, but she doesn't say a single word as she retrieves two towels and offers me a hand out of the tub. There is, however, a challenge in her green eyes. Not submission.

And why not? I've talked a good game, but I'm fighting not to hide in the tub like a coward. It takes everything I have to lift my hand and place it into hers. She guides me easily up and holds firm as I step out onto the tiled floor. Somehow, I'm not even remotely surprised to find it's heated. The room itself is balmy, but after the warmth of the water, it feels cool enough to prickle my skin and draw my nipples into hard points.

Maura's gaze drops to my chest, and she licks her lips. It seems to be an involuntary gesture, which only makes it sexier.

No matter what else is true, I affect her just as deeply as she affects me.

I'm still trying to decide how to handle that when she swings the towel around me and gets to work drying my body. She does a good job at first—she whisks the water off my arms and spends entirely too much time on my breasts, lifting and weighing them in her toweled hands—but as she drops to her knees before me, she seems to forget what she's about.

Truth be told, I forget too.

Maura runs her hands on the outside of my thighs and stops at my hips. When she speaks, her voice is hoarse with need. "Lie down on the bed, Jules. Once I start, I'm not going to want to stop. We can't have you falling and cracking your head. It would ruin a good afternoon and an even better night."

I want to tell her that she's being arrogant, but my knees are already feeling a little shaky, and she hasn't even put her mouth on me yet. I have to focus to keep my legs from buckling as I move around her to perch on the bed. I half expect Maura to follow me, but she merely rotates to keep me in sight.

I can't stand this distance between us. I don't know how to broach it with words, but I *do* know how to incite action. I prop my hands behind me and lean back a little, arching my back. Then I hold her eyes as I slowly spread my thighs in clear invitation.

Still, Maura doesn't move. It's like she's frozen in place. I'm so tense from this moment out of time that I can't stop shaking. I clear my throat. "I told you what I want, Maura. Don't make me say it again."

A little smile curves Maura's lips. It's the only warning I get before she starts crawling to me. It should be awkward and painful to watch, but somehow she makes it graceful and so sexy, I can't catch my breath.

"This is what you wanted, isn't it?" She kneels between my

legs and rubs her cheek against my inner thigh. "Me, on my knees. Paying penance for the wrongs I've done to you."

"That's not what I—"

She presses her mouth to my pussy before I can finish the protest. In the bath, she obviously intended to tease me until I lost my mind. The tension between us has changed now. It's different than last time, too. Back on the ship, she ate my pussy like she'd never get a chance to taste me again. That's not what she's doing right now. No, her mouth moves on me like a promise.

I'm afraid to contemplate what the promise might be.

Instead, I give myself fully over to the pleasure. There will be plenty of time to worry and wonder tomorrow. Right now, all I want to do is take what she's giving me with no questions asked.

It's almost as if that decision unlocks something inside me. Maura's next lick sends pleasure cascading through me. I dig my fingers into the bedding and cry out as I come.

It doesn't stop for a long, long time.

13

MAURA

Juliette sleeps like she's never shared a bed, sprawled out and snoring softly. I find it strangely endearing, but then, I find everything about her endearing right now. We didn't manage to talk yesterday or last night, but that's fine. No matter what else is true, Juliette and I are drawn to each other. All the words and noble notions got in the way of that, but it's over now.

She's mine.

I'm hers.

All that's left is to figure out the details.

I'm not remotely surprised to find our clothing was laundered while we were distracted. I take a few seconds to check my pockets and weapons, but nothing is missing or blatantly tampered with. It doesn't mean whoever did our laundry *didn't* go through it—I'd be surprised if that were the case—but at least they didn't steal from us.

After a quick glance at Juliette, I judge her to still be sleeping deeply. She likely won't wake until I give her reason to, which means I have time to arrange for breakfast. Eloise mentioned it in passing when I booked the room. It's not an inn, so I suspect the rates are significantly steeper than they would be otherwise, but there was no way I'd have convinced Juliette to leave this building yesterday.

A small price to pay for how things worked out.

I get dressed and slip out of the room. Last night, this place was loud and busy and buzzing with energy. This morning... Morning? I eye the bright light streaming in from the open doors. Maybe it's afternoon.

Either way, everything is more muted now. There are a few people at the tables in various stages of undress, but it's impossible to tell if they threw on whatever was handy to come down or if they've been here this entire time.

I make my way carefully down the stairs and cross to the bar. Eloise is behind it, looking as fresh as a daisy. She gives me a lecherous grin. "Seems you made good use of the room."

Against all reason, I have to fight not to blush. I clear my throat. "I was wondering about breakfast."

"You know we're not an inn, girl." She rolls her eyes, but her smile is still wide. "I'll have Nadia bring up something in a little while."

I almost tell her to send someone else, but the truth is that this *isn't* an inn. I slip her two gold pieces. "Thank you."

She eyes the coins. "You're trying to buy my goodwill, and I don't dislike it. That girl really has you wrapped around her little finger, doesn't she?"

"You have no idea." I glance up at the door to the room where she still sleeps. "She's the love of my life."

"Glad you got that figured out. I thought you were going to make an ass of yourself yesterday and make me throw you out." She tsks. "Jealousy is a fine thing to flavor fucking, but too much will ruin a relationship."

I raise my brows. "I will strive to keep that in mind."

"Good girl." She half turns, and if I thought her smile was

real enough for me, it's nothing compared to the way she brightens. "Well, hello there, stranger."

"Eloise." The voice is deep and rough. "It's been a long time."

She leans on the bar and twines a strand of white hair around her finger, as coquettish as a woman a fraction of her age. "Never thought I'd see you around *these* parts, boy. I know how your people feel about the island."

I freeze as the speaker comes even with me and leans wearily against the counter. It's not his height or the broadness of his shoulders that makes my mouth go dry with fear. No, that fault lies entirely with the crimson cloak draped around his shoulders.

Cŵn Annwn.

He sighs, seemingly oblivious to the way I've gone tense. "I'm on a retrieval mission, if you can believe it. Someone was foolish enough to steal from one of ours."

"Is that so?" Eloise flicks a glance at me, and I am struck by the sudden suspicion that she knows *exactly* what was stolen and by whom.

I drop my hand casually to the dagger at my waist. Cŵn Annwn might have been more myth than real to me until this point, but the man standing next to me is breathing the same air I am.

Which means he can die.

"Will your crew be joining you on this hunt?" Eloise is still flirting up a storm, but some tension has bled into her tone. "You know the monarch won't like that, Bowen."

"I'm aware." His voice deepens a bit, going harsh. "They may be allowed to run this monstrosity for reasons unknown, but that doesn't mean I answer to them."

"You do on this island." She straightens. "I highly suggest you present yourself to them, sooner rather than later. It'd be such a shame if this became an inter-realm incident. You're too pretty for the creative punishments they come up with when they're inspired."

Bowen grimaces. "It's already an inter-realm incident."

"Mmm. It's not the same and you know it. I suppose you'll be wanting a room."

"Better here than the inn. More people coming and going."

She makes a point of eyeing his crimson cloak. "You stand out, boy. And I'm not talking about the pretty face."

No matter what the witch says, he's not pretty. His features are too brutal for that. Square jaw, large crooked nose, strong brows, and intense dark eyes. His long dark hair likely reaches his shoulders when it's not tied back from his face. Scars mark his knuckles and the backs of his hands. Defensive wounds similar to those that mar my own skin. A fighter, but I didn't need to see the scars to recognize that.

The sword at his waist tells me everything I need to know. It's a style I can't identify, much heftier than mine, and sheathed in a scabbard of leather, worn from time and exposure to the elements at sea. It's not the scabbard of a nobleman, crusted with jewels and only there to be pretty. He *uses* that sword, and has for a long time.

I have to get Juliette out of here, and I have to do it now. I clear my throat. "Breakfast?"

"It'll be up shortly." Eloise winks at me, which could mean anything. Part of me hesitates to leave her alone with the Cŵn Annwn, but the truth is that she could sell us out even if I'm standing right there. I can't do anything to stop it.

Better that I escape with Juliette.

Even as I start for the stairs, working to keep my pace measured and relaxed, my mind is racing. If it were a matter of returning the piece of eight, I'd do it myself, but the Cŵn Annwn don't have a reputation for being forgiving. Juliette stole from them and then used that stolen item to travel to *Atlantis*, which is already a sore spot with them just for existing.

They'll make an example of her—a deadly one.

I move through the door and shut it softly behind me. One deep breath and then I'm hurrying to the side of the bed. I press a hand lightly to Juliette's mouth. "Wake up."

I expect her to blink and stretch and ease into wakefulness. She doesn't. She opens her eyes, seemingly completely coherent. It's a neat trick, one I was forced to learn after a good number of nights when my life was in danger. I don't like that she's had to learn it as well, but that's something to deal with another day.

I lean down and whisper, "One of the Cŵn Annwn is here, hunting for a thief." She starts to sit up, but I press her back down. "*Here*, Jules. In this building. Downstairs."

She narrows her eyes. It's a clear order to remove my hand, but I only do so reluctantly. Juliette sits up slowly. "You're serious."

"Yes." At least she's matching my tone, keeping her voice soft. "He's not an old geezer. He's a big guy, and he moves like he murders for a living. I'm not entirely sure I can take him." I could if he's human and doesn't have magic—most human bodies are comprised of enough water that I can use my powers to slow them. But I can't guarantee either of those things.

Juliette eyes the door in a truly worrisome way, but she sighs and looks at me before I can do something like grab her arm. "I don't suppose I can just give it back?"

"I think that ship has sailed."

"That's what I'm afraid of."

At this point, I don't even know if leaving Atlantis and going back to our realm would solve things. All I know of the Cŵn Annwn is rumors and myths and a few drunken sailors' ghost tales. How much is real? I can't bargain Juliette's safety on hoping the stories were at all fictional.

Even going back to the ship isn't a good solution. *The Kelpie* may be faster than any ship in our realm, but when you open up that category into all realms that ever existed... Who knows what kind of magic this hunter has? Not to mention we still don't have a spell to ensure our safe exit from Atlantis.

No. We'll have to take this in steps.

"First, we need to get out of here without him seeing us."

I expect Juliette to argue with me, but for once she doesn't. She nods, her skin taking on a waxy tone. When she speaks, there's a tremor in her voice. "The hunter in my father's court really wanted to impress some of the courtiers. I wasn't supposed to overhear, but he went into great detail about what they did to someone who was trespassing between realms and refused to join his crew." She swallows visibly. "I don't think I'm up for deadly torture."

"*No one* is going to torture you." I take her hand and squeeze. "I will kill them all myself before I let them touch you."

She gives a wobbly smile. "Always sailing to my rescue, huh?"

Now probably isn't the time to say it, but with danger knocking at our door, I refuse to let anything else go unsaid between us. I lift her hand to my mouth and press a kiss to her knuckles. "I will always save you, Jules. I will always come for you, And I will always keep you safe. I know I've done a shitty job of proving that in the past couple of days, but it's the truth."

"Maura, nothing has really changed about our circum-stances. "

Nothing has changed...except everything has changed. "I'll explain everything once I get us both to safety. But I'm going to need you to trust me in the meantime and do as I say. Can you do that?"

Juliette looks like she wants to argue but seems to catch herself before any words leave her lips. Finally, she nods. "This only applies to us escaping certain death and torture right now, today. Don't expect unquestioning obedience from me as a general rule."

Despite everything, I chuckle. "Arguing with you is one of my favorite hobbies, Jules. I wouldn't give that up for anything." I tug her gently to her feet. "Now get dressed, and do it quickly."

For once, she obeys. She's just gotten her dress pulled over her head when someone knocks on the door. Juliette yanks her clothing into place and gives me a scared look. I motion for her to move to the corner, out of sight. Once she's in place, I crack open the door.

Nadia stands a few feet back, a tray with a metal-covered plate perched on one generous hip. She arches a brow at me. "Expecting someone else?"

She knows. Which means Eloise knows as well. I suspected as much, but getting confirmation leaves me cold. We are on a tiny island where we don't know the rules and have no safe way to leave. An island opposed to the very definition of what Cŵn Annwn are. Atlantis would be smart to serve us up on a platter to them.

It's what I would do in their place.

14

JULIETTE

It's only when Maura looks over at me, her green eyes a little too wide, that I realize she's scared. I don't think I've ever seen Maura afraid before.

She takes a deep breath and shuts it all down. It's honestly impressive and a little scary. One moment she's obviously fighting to figure out what to do, and the next she appears cool and calm.

"Would you like to come in, Nadia?"

I jolt a little. I thought the voice outside the room sounded familiar, but I hadn't realized it was Nadia. It seems too big a coincidence, but what do I know? Maybe her job is delivering food to patrons who stay overnight.

Maura steps back just enough to allow the other woman in but uses her body to block my sight through the open door.

And to block anyone from seeing me.

Nadia walks to the small table tucked against a side wall, seemingly unconcerned with the fact she's presented Maura with her back and Maura is touching her sword in a clear threat. She sets the tray down and turns to face us. "Well, this is a right mess."

"Speak fast, or I'll slit your throat."

"*Maura.*"

Nadia raises her brows. "You'd never make it off the island alive. Eloise is protective of her people."

I shiver. "Maura, that's enough. I know we're in a bad spot, but that doesn't change the fact there's no way the..." I pause. I'm not one to cleave to superstitious fears, but it seems a bad idea to name the group hunting me. "He can't know what I look like. We walk out the front door and keep walking."

"It's a gamble, and I won't gamble with your life. There are portraits of you all over that castle, and if the old bastard hunter knows who stole from him, it's easy enough to pass along one of those with the news of the theft. That's not even getting into magical means of tracking." Maura shakes her head sharply. "We're leaving, but we're doing it stealthily."

Nadia props her hands on her hips. "I have a suggestion."

"More like a trap," Maura snaps.

I swallow my frustration. Maura is only trying to protect me, and I very much do not want to die. I can't pretend I've been in many situations where my life was at risk. There were the assassination attempts a few months back, but my father took care of those and then removed me as heir. After that, I wasn't worth enough to murder. They left their mark, though. I don't sleep nearly as deeply as I used to.

Nadia seems entirely unaffected by Maura's animosity. "If Eloise wanted to hand you over, she would have done it while you were distracted downstairs. You'd be a fool to reject help right now."

"Maura, she's right." I keep my voice even. I was distantly aware that stealing from the Cŵn Annwn was a risk, but it had barely felt real. It *still* doesn't feel real, but I'm not foolish enough to wait until there's a literal sword over my neck before I take things seriously. "We need help. Unless we want to take our chances on a portal or sailing away without the exit spell in place, we can't do this alone."

Maura curses and spins to face Nadia. "Fine. I'm listening."

"Bowen has to present himself to the monarch and get permission to hunt on the island. He's leaving shortly, which will give you time to slip out."

"What about his crew? Surely he didn't come here alone."

"Of course not." Nadia smiles, the expression cold and unlike the warm, teasing woman I met last night. "But Atlanteans don't take kindly to the Cŵn Annwn stomping over what's ours. It makes people nervous, and nervous people do foolish and violent things. His crew will stay on his ship for the duration of the hunt on the island." She shrugs. "The same can't be said for open water. The sooner you leave, the better."

It's a lot to take in.

I swallow hard. "But the monarch will let...Bowen...hunt on the island?"

"Yes," she says simply. "There's an arrangement that goes back beyond memory. The hunters leave us in peace and preserve something of a sanctuary here for inter-realm travelers. But the trade-off for that freedom is that when they come hunting a specific person, permission is usually granted as a courtesy."

Well, shit. I kind of hoped since the monarch seems to like me, they might hesitate to let me be hunted and potentially murdered on the island. It was a long shot anyway.

In the distance, there's a tinkling of many small bells. Nadia smooths back her hair. "He's left. Gather your things, and I'll take you to the back door."

Maura's already moving, slipping her many weapons back into place. It feels a bit like magic, watching them disappear. I don't understand how she's carrying so many.

"Can you secure us an exit spell?" she asks without turning around.

Nadia shakes her head. "No. Eloise prefers to stay out of that thread of business, and none of her people will cross that decision. Your best bet is Seiko at The Siren's Call, the bar down the street. Very few people on the island will turn you over to the Cŵn Annwn if they have any other choice, but she has a particular vendetta against them. She'll give you a good deal."

Maura nods and turns for the door, but gratitude has me crossing to Nadia and taking her hands. "Thank you."

"Don't worry, love. You're paying for the privilege." She gives me a saucy wink. "One other thing."

"We have to *go*."

"Hold on, Maura."

Nadia lifts the metal plate covering, revealing that there's not actually food under there. Instead, two cloaks are neatly folded. One is a deep green and the other is a gray that feels muted in a way that may be magic. I pick it up and run my fingers over the fine weave. "I don't suppose this will have eyes sliding right off me?"

Nadia laughs. "You can't afford that kind of magic. No, this is simply playing with perception. Cloaked strangers aren't uncommon here." She takes it from my hands and sweeps it over my shoulders in a practiced move. "Keep your hood up, love."

Maura doesn't exactly shoulder between us, but she appears at my side, close enough to brush against my body as she grabs the green cloak. "How much?"

"You've already paid." She laughs. "Or did you think we're so greedy as to take *two gold* for food?"

Maura opens her mouth, hesitates, and then shakes her head. "Damn."

"Indeed." Nadia moves to the door and pokes her head out. A few seconds later, she looks back at us. "Let's go."

Maura grabs my arm. "Stay close." Her voice is low and dangerous. "No matter what happens, I will get you out of this."

I don't tell her that we can trust Nadia. I met the woman last night, for only a few minutes. I have no idea if she's trustworthy or not, but it's clear her patroness is playing a deeper game. In the end, we don't have a choice. We have to trust her.

At least long enough to get out of this building.

I expect Nadia to lead us to the main staircase that circles the exterior wall. Instead, she goes in the opposite direction. I can't help glancing nervously over the railing that gives a view of the whole main floor. There are a handful of pirates already drinking and laughing at the tables. One of them starts to look up, but a person begins to sing a soft, hunting melody on the other side of the room. All attention shifts to them, and the laughter quiets.

I jolt when a hand slips into mine but relax when I realize it's Maura. She tugs me along behind her as we follow Nadia past half a dozen rooms with varying color doors to one that is indistinguishable from the others, aside from being yellow.

I expect to find us in a staircase or some kind of staff room, but it seems to be a working room similar to the one we just exited. It's decorated yellow to match the door, its four-poster bed cheery and bright in a way that should be off-putting but instead makes me want to throw myself in the middle of it. A neat trick, that.

Nadia bypasses the bed and heads directly to a large wardrobe positioned against an interior wall. She gives me a saucy grin and throws it open. Immediately, all sorts of fabrics explode from the space. It takes me a few seconds to realize they are all dresses in a rainbow of colors and fabrics and styles. Truly, there are enough to fit three wardrobes, all stuffed into the single one.

"I am not putting on one of those." Maura takes a step back

as if Nadia will try to wrestle her into one of the offending garments.

"No, of course not. This is only to discourage patrons from investigating further." Nadia motions us closer. "Here, come help me."

It takes both me and Nadia to pull the dresses away from the center, revealing a dark gap in the wall. If this is a hole for an assassin to sneak through, I don't see how they would be successful unless their target was blackout drunk and passed out. Similarly, all the dresses must muffle sound, so this would be a terrible place to spy from. There's only one purpose this can serve, and it's the one we're using it for right now.

To escape.

"There's a staircase that will take you down to the back. Be quiet; the walls are very thin, and Ray's song will only last another few minutes. Our lot isn't the most perceptive, but there's no reason to take chances. The locals will not side with the Cŵn Annwn, but a pirate is a pirate, and there are plenty who would like to be owed a favor by the inter-realm hunters."

"We'll be careful." I impulsively pull Nadia into a hug. "Thank you so much for all your help, and I don't just mean this morning."

"Take care of yourself, Juliette." She releases me and steps back, turning her attention to Maura. "And you...take care of the princess. If you don't realize what a gem she is, then someone else will steal her from you."

"I. Am. Aware."

Nadia smiles slowly. "Now you are."

Maura insists on my going first into the wardrobe. I don't think she trusts Nadia not to slam the door shut and whisk me away. I won't pretend I don't enjoy her jealousy, just a little bit. Or at least I would if we weren't in fear of our lives. Or, rather, *my* life. The hunter isn't after Maura. He's after me. She could wash her hands of this whole mess right now and leave me to figure it out for myself.

She won't.

I don't know what the future holds for us, but I can't believe things are unchanged after what happened last night. She held me like she loved me. She touched me in a way that didn't feel like goodbye but more like a promise of the future.

A future with us together.

Maybe I'm naive to believe that, but I can't shake it. And so I climb through the wardrobe and into the darkness.

15

MAURA

"The Siren's Call is on the other side of the square. It's the biggest building." Nadia huffs out a breath. "Now *go*."

"Thank you." After that, there's nothing left to say. I go.

I wrestle my way through the wardrobe and into the narrow gap at the back. The stairway is broad enough that I don't have to angle my body to avoid my scabbard scraping on the wall. I can hear Juliette a few steps down, her breathing choppy.

It's only then that I remember she doesn't like tight, closed spaces.

I hurry down the last few steps between us and feel for her hand. "It's okay." The words are barely a whisper. I am *very* aware that we can hear faint voices through the wall on our right. Which means they can hear us, too. "I've got you."

She doesn't respond with words. Instead, she clamps her hand around mine and holds tight. We inch carefully down the stairs. Even though the Cŵn Annwn is supposedly gone, the air of danger has tightened around me. We have to get off this fucking island, and we have to do it right now.

It takes a small eternity to make it to the ground level. I pull

Juliette close. "Let me go first." She huffs in exasperation but nods, edging to the side so I can slip past.

As promised, the door leads out the back of the brothel. There are a few buildings back here, but the forest creeps in close enough that no one should be able to see us. I still hold my breath and wait several beats, half sure that we're about to step into an ambush. I know it doesn't make sense. If Eloise wanted to hand us over, she would have done it already.

Unless she didn't want a mess in her precious brothel.

I draw one of my medium-sized knives on instinct. It's small enough that I can conceal it within my duster but plenty large enough to carve our way through anyone who gets between us and our escape.

"Maura?"

I shake myself. "I think we're good. Come on."

It would be preferable to take cover in the trees, but I haven't forgotten the warning about portals. I'm not even sure what portals look like on this island, so I can't guarantee that we wouldn't fall into one if we crossed the tree line. The messiness of the situation only gets worse as time goes on. I haven't even begun to consider how we get to the dock and row out toward the ship without anyone seeing us. There has to be a way, but without that spell to exit Atlantis safely, it's a lost cause.

What I need is Daichi. I didn't see him in The Bawdy Banquet last night, but admittedly I was more focused on getting to Juliette before she disappeared with Nadia than I was about searching in the room for my navigator. Now it's too late.

The buildings are situated close together, but they aren't fully connected, so I can see down the narrow alley to the square. From how loud things were last night, I half expected to see people passed out in the dirt this afternoon, but it looks just the same as it did when we arrived. People move to and fro, some quickly and intent on their destination, and some leisurely as if they have all the time in the world. Unfortunately, there are not enough people to constitute a crowd that we could hide in.

"We'll go along the back of the buildings and come around the other side." I squeeze Juliette's hand. "It will be okay."

"You keep saying that. Are you trying to calm me or yourself?" Juliette smiles, and it strikes me that *she* is the one actually reassuring *me*. I should remind her exactly what danger she's in, but I appreciate the reassurance.

"Maybe a bit of both." There's no time left for talking, so I lead the way down the back of the buildings. Every step, I expect that crimson-cloaked bastard to pop out and threaten us. Somehow, making it to the end of the buildings is almost worse. My tension is so thick, I could cut it with my sword. I hesitate. I don't want to let Juliette out of my sight, but if he knows what she looks like, it's not safe for her to wander about where anyone can see her.

She's not going to like this. "I need you to stay here."

"Absolutely fucking not." She yanks her hand out of mine. "I'm not going to sit around and hide while you put yourself in danger."

"That is exactly what I expect you to do." I take her shoulders and wait for her to meet my gaze. "Danger is what I do, Jules. I'm more equipped to deal with it than anyone. Let me secure this exit spell for our ship, and then we'll sail out of here and never look back. He'll have no reason to come after you if we drop that piece of eight into his pocket and return to our realm."

"Maura." Her eyes shine a little strangely. "You just said *our ship*."

I did, didn't I? What a strange little slip, but it fills me with warmth. Last night I promised myself I would stop fighting this, but it still feels a little odd to look into a future where Juliette is at my side. Where I can sail from one side of our realm to the other, showing her all the secret little paradises I found over the past ten years.

No, my ship is not a castle, and my crew will hardly dance in attendance the way her staff did, but maybe I need to start giving Juliette the benefit of the doubt. And believing her when she says this is what she wants.

"I did."

"Do you mean it?" For once, there's none of her bravado or cheery chaos present. This is the Jules I fell in love with ten years ago, soft and sweet and so filled with hope that it makes my heart ache. "Really mean it?"

"Yes. But I need you to stay here and stay safe so we can make that a reality. Can you do that for me, Jules? Promise me."

She doesn't look happy, but she nods all the same. "I'll stay here, but don't you think it's a little strange for me to be lurking? Won't it raise suspicion?" She asks it so innocently, but I see right through her.

The problem is that she's right. There's no one behind the buildings, which was ideal when we were sneaking, but sneaking meant we were on the move. Standing around is hardly stealthy.

I worry at my bottom lip. I can't take her into the inn with me. If I were the hunter, that's the first place I would start questioning people. Juliette is beautiful and vivacious, so people are guaranteed to remember her. I look around, searching for a good solution.

My answer comes in the form of whistles and squawks. I barely registered the sounds previously because I was so focused on the threat of attack. Now I wonder how I could've missed them in the first place. They seem to be coming from the building we're standing next to. I frown. "Is that a...parrot shop?"

Juliette's eyes light up. "I could wait in there. I didn't even realize parrot shops were a thing."

Truth be told, I didn't realize it either. There's a strange sort of mythos that says pirates and parrots go together, but when you're spending weeks and weeks at sea, any animal that is not serving a purpose is a liability. At this point, we don't even keep a cat on board because we have spells to ward against rodents. And parrots live for decades.

I weigh my options, but really, it's no choice at all. Juliette can't stand around, appearing to lurk, without drawing attention to herself. But a shopper, taking her time and browsing the wares? That's a thing that exists everywhere. Even here. Probably especially here, since there are plenty of things your average pirate does not see every day.

All that being said, there's one last thing to address. "That will work, under one condition."

She blinks those big dark eyes at me, the very picture of innocence. "What condition?"

"You will not, under any circumstances, purchase one or more parrots."

Her innocent look takes on an element of mischievousness. It's in the twinkle of her eyes and the curve of her lips. It means trouble. That doesn't stop me from wanting to kiss the look right off her face. Juliette grins. "What makes you think I'm going to purchase a parrot?"

"Call it a hunch."

If anything, her grin widens. "I could teach it to sound like me, and we could use it as a diversion."

I am nearly certain she's teasing me and doesn't mean it. But not 100 percent certain. "Promise me, Jules."

"Fine." She rolls her eyes. "If you insist on being reasonable and taking all the fun out of the situation, I promise not to purchase one or more parrots."

I'm not sure I believe her, but it will have to do because we're out of time. I peek around the corner of the parrot shop and eye the square. It's much the same as the last time I looked, with people meandering about. There isn't a crimson cloak in sight. We won't get a better chance than this. "You go first. Walk purposely and keep your hood up."

"I do know how to move around unnoticed, you know. I used to do it all the time around the palace. How do you think I snuck out to see you all those times?"

Truth be told, I hadn't thought about it in all that much detail. I was simply so astounded that she kept returning. Every time I went to our meeting spot, I expected her not to show. The princess of Skoiya and the poor little orphan girl? That may be a romance worthy of an epic poem, but epic poems are fiction.

And yet she always came. I would look up, and she would be there in front of me, her smile colored with joy and maybe a little bit of relief. As if she wasn't quite sure I would be here this time, either.

It's funny how I convinced myself I could leave her behind for good. It's the most accomplished lie I've ever told.

I hook an arm around her waist and pull her into me. Juliette barely has time to make a surprised noise when I take her mouth. I keep fucking up my words, but I have never fucked up this. I kiss her with all the things I keep failing to speak, and when I finally lift my head, it turns out there's really only one thing I need to say. "I love you."

"I love you, too." She's breathless and flushed. I like her like that, but I can't enjoy the sight, not until I know she's safe.

"Go. Be careful."

"I will." She brushes a soft, sweet kiss to my lips. And then she's gone.

I lean against the side of the building and watch her make her way to the door. She does exactly as I instructed, walking with her shoulders straight and her face angled away from the square. Within several racing beats of my heart, she disappears through the door to the parrot shop. I force myself to wait another minute or two before I amble past the shop and slip through the doors of the bar.

I almost expected something as magical and over the top as I've seen in other parts of this island, but this bar looks like exactly what it is. A bar. It's a little lighter and airier than a lot of others I've been in, and it certainly cleaner, but the worn wooden bar could've been at home in a thousand others like it. My shoulders relax a fraction from sheer familiarity. I can do this. I have coaxed vital bits of information from more bartenders than I care to count. They hear everything, and the first place sailors stop when they've made landfall is either the brothel or the bar.

If there's one thing sailors like to do, it's brag. As a result, bartenders are the best informants a pirate captain can ask for. Most of them can be purchased for the right price, too.

I make it three steps into the room, carried by that feeling of familiarity, before my brain catches up with what my eyes already noticed. The bar itself isn't the only familiar thing in this room. The man leaning against it, in an almost identical position to what he took up this morning, is the hunter.

Fuck.

16

MAURA

I almost back right out the door. We need the exit spell, but there are other ways to get it, and those ways won't involve interacting with the Cŵn Annwn again. It's too late, though. He looks up and sees me before I take the first step.

Fuck.

There's nothing for it. I move casually to the bar but make no effort to take the spot next to him. The room is half full, but most people seem to be nursing a hangover instead of pursuing a new one. It's all blurry eyes and slumped postures. The bartender alone seems immune, moving behind the bar with a pep in her step and a bright smile.

She turns that smile on me as I take a spot as close to the door as possible. She's a pretty one. Her long, straight dark hair is shaved on one side, revealing a delicately pointed ear. A half elf. Her coloring is much more human than River's, her skin pale and her eyes as dark as her hair. She's dressed in pants, a perfectly tailored shirt, and suspenders. When she speaks, her voice is low and throaty. "What can I get you, lovely?"

Even knowing the bartenders tend to come in only a few

different varieties, and flirty is just as common as cranky, I'm not entirely unaffected. Or maybe it's the watching Cŵn Annwn who makes me so nervous. I try for a smile, but I'm not sure I pull it off. "I'll start with a drink. Whatever's best here."

"You again." To my horror, Bowen slides his drink down the bar and moves closer to me. Were this anyone else, I might think he was attempting to hit on me, but there's a keen look in his eyes that speaks to a wolf on the hunt.

"Me again." I watch the bartender pour a frothy pink drink into a pristine mug. What the fuck did I order? There's no time to worry about it. I shift to face Bowen. When in doubt, go on the attack. "Are you following me?"

"Should I be?" Again, the words could be flirty coming from any other mouth, but from him they sound like a threat. He stares at me with those cold dark eyes as if he can read my very thoughts. The concept is alarming, because that magic certainly does exist. Oh gods, can he read my mind? I work to keep my surface thoughts placid.

This is a fucking mess.

"If you're looking for a romp, you're destined to be disappointed. I don't appreciate the company of men."

He narrows his eyes. "That's not what I'm here for."

"Here you go, lovely." The bartender slides my drink in front of me with another of those charming grins. "It's the house special, made from fruit you won't find anywhere around here...or anywhere else." She gives Bowen a smug look. "Isn't that right, Cŵn Annwn?"

"Your monarch can't protect you if you continue to provoke me."

The bartender's smile goes sharp and almost predatory. "I think you'll find they can do exactly that. You shouldn't be here, little dog. You should've presented yourself to the court by now. Your hunt is not sanctioned."

His jaw goes tight. "We have a treaty."

"The treaty requires certain steps...that you are not following."

The hairs on my arms stand on end. I look slowly around the room to find everyone is watching this interaction. Where before people seemed tired and perfectly willing to go about their own business and ignore us, now they are all staring daggers in Bowen's back. Nadia was right; he has no friends here. One of the people at the nearest table carefully draws a stiletto knife and sets it on the worn wood. A clear threat.

Not that Bowen seems to care.

I spend half a second wondering what it must be like to move through the world that sure of your superiority. What kind of magic must this man wield?

I'm powerful, but there is always a tipping point where the sheer number of bodies in a fight overwhelms anyone's power. They are easily twenty people in this room. If they all joined the fight, I would be taken down within a minute or two. Bowen hasn't even turned around to survey the threat.

"I am looking for a woman."

The bartender smirks. "The brothel is down the square. We don't trade in sex here. Eloise doesn't like other businesses stepping on her toes, and we work very hard not to piss Eloise off."

Again, he clenches his jaw. That can't be good for his teeth. Bowen straightens. Back in the brothel, I hadn't realized exactly how big he is. This man is a fucking monster. I'm tall, but he overshoots me by a head and shoulders. His reach must be deadly, especially with a long-ass sword.

To her credit, the bartender doesn't flinch. She merely raises a pristine black brow. "Come back after you've gone to court, Cŵn Annwn. "

The silence stretches, pregnant with the possibility of violence, and I find myself holding my breath. If a fight breaks out, do I stay and engage? Or do I run and hope no one realizes I'm running back to Juliette? There are no good answers.

Damn it, I need the exit spell.

"When I come back, you *will* answer my questions."

"Only if you ask them nicely," the bartender says sweetly.

Bowen curses. He shoves away from the bar, gives me a long look, and then stalks out. The door swings shut behind him, and there's a beat when everyone seems to be holding their breath, waiting to see if he'll return. He doesn't.

I turn back to the bar with an exhale of relief, only to find the bartender watching me closely. She props her elbows on the shining wood and gives me a gentle smile. "You've had dealings with the Cŵn Annwn in the past. Most people don't recognize the danger they bring."

"That's not a question." I take a sip of my frothy pink drink, and I'm surprised to find it's actually quite good.

I must make a face, because she laughs. "You're not from around here."

"Is anyone from around here?"

"No, not really." She gives me a long look. "You came in in here with a lot of purpose for someone who only wants a drink. What can I help you with?"

There's a part of me that doesn't even want to ask for the exit spell. This woman is obviously no friend of the Cŵn Annwn, but that doesn't mean she's a friend of mine. With that said, Nadia sent us here, and even if I don't trust her entirely, there *has* to be a way to get off this fucking island. I take another drink. "I need an exit spell for my ship."

The bartender's eyes light up. "Oh, I see." She leans back and seems to do some mental calculations. "How big a ship and how many people?"

"I don't see how that matters. A spell's a spell."

She shakes her head slowly. "You know better, Captain. No spell is identical, not with so many components at play, an exit spell from Atlantis is doubly complicated. I need that information, ten gold pieces of whatever currency your realm carries, and three days' time."

I flinch. "The information and price I can do, but that time-line won't work for me."

"That's too damn bad. The timeline is what the timeline is." She shrugs. "I'm willing to give you a room on the house for the duration, but only because I like you."

"Not because you're making a killing on the spell?"

She grins. "Well, there is that, too."

Could I hide Juliette here for three days? It seems improbable, especially if Bowen is sniffing around, asking questions. Someone will talk. *No, this won't work. There has to be another way.*

"You're thinking that there must be another way." When I look at the bartender in surprise, she shrugs again. "They all think that. The ones who end up in Atlantis by mistake, I mean."

"Who says I ended up here by mistake?"

"Call it a hunch. Look, I'm not trying to fuck with you. The money lender will charge you a third more, and you can throw yourself on the mercy of the monarch, but if you've met them, you know there's not much mercy to be found. No matter which route you take, the timeline will be the same. It sounds like you're in trouble. I'm your best bet."

There has to be a better way to go about this, but I'm coming up short on options. This island is not large enough to dodge a hunter for three days. The square is only so big, and there are only so many businesses and buildings to hide in. Our best bet may be the forest, but that presents its own dangers. If I have to choose between a portal to a mysterious realm or facing down the Cŵn Annwn, I honestly don't know which is the preferable path.

Juliette is depending on me to keep her safe. I can't fail her now. Not again. I'll just have to make it work.

I force a smile. "Three days, a free room, and five gold pieces."

"Oh, I like you. I'll give it to you for eight because you're entertaining, but don't test my goodwill by asking for less."

"Deal." I detail out the specs of my ship and crew. It's nothing more than anyone looking at *The Kelpie* could figure out on their own, but it feels like a risk all the same. "And the room?"

The bartender reaches under the bar and comes up with a small key. She passes it to me. "Last room at the end of the hallway. There's a door in the back for those who want to be...discreet."

Gods, I hope this isn't a trap. "Thanks." I palm the key and step back. "I'll come around later and check on things." Not that I even know what to check on when it comes to a spell of this nature. Transportation spells are some of the trickiest bits of magic in existence. If something goes wrong, it goes horrifically, nightmarishly, fatally wrong.

It's only as I back toward the door that I realize I have no idea if Bowen actually went to the court or if he continued what was apparently a search of the businesses in the square. If he did the latter, that means his next stop was...

The parrot shop.

I turn without another word and walk out of the bar. It's everything I can do not to run, but I don't want to draw attention to myself if my suspicions are wrong. Everything looks much the same as it did a few minutes ago when I walked in, but that doesn't mean anything. Neither does the fact Bowen obviously has no friends here on the island.

He doesn't need friends to kill the love of my life.

I keep my pace slow and measured as I walk to the door of the parrot shop. I'm not sure what I expect when I walk through but the sight that greets me stops me in my tracks. This room is a riot of colors, some that seem to defy comprehension.

There are birds everywhere. They sit on the fake branches that circle the room, they perch on edges carved into the wall, and a trio of them alight on the wide-brimmed hat of the person chatting with Juliette.

A smiling, happy, healthy Juliette.

She turns to me, delight written across her features. "Maura, there you are. This is Kai. They're the owner of the shop. Isn't it delightful?"

Delightful is certainly one way to describe it. It seems like hell on earth to me. I can't help hunching my shoulders as several parrots fly overhead, certain one of them is going to take a shit on me. "Juliette." I have to work to keep my voice even and unworried. "It's time to go."

She narrows her eyes, but something must show on my face because she nods instead of argues. Juliette turns to the parrot shop's owner with a charming smile. "Thank you so much for keeping me company. It was absolutely lovely chatting with you."

"Of course." They smile. "Please come back and visit before you leave the island."

"I absolutely will."

I turn and fall into step next to her as we leave the shop. It only takes a few seconds to bring her up to speed. I clasp her arm and guide her back the way we came, near the tree line. "I need you to stay in the room so I can track down Daichi and update the crew."

"Okay."

I'm already starting to detail out my argument on why she needs to stay in the room when I realize she agreed with me. "Really?"

"Yes." Juliette smiles, but her eyes are worried. "I know you think I'm reckless, but I occasionally do know when to quit. I don't want to die, Maura. I'll do whatever you tell me to. For now, at least."

I don't want her afraid, but if that's what it takes for her to stay safe, then it is a small price to pay. All the same, I take her hand and raise it to my lips, then press a kiss to her knuckles. "Three days. We just need to hold out for three days, and then we get off this island."

She watches me with sober eyes. "And then we'll be together."

It's not a question, but it feels a little bit like she's asking me to confirm. "Yes, Jules. And then will be together. Forever."

17

JULIETTE

After Maura tucks me safely away in the room, she leaves to track down her navigator so she can send a message to her crew to be ready to leave at a moment's notice. A first, she wants to take the piece of eight with her in case the Cŵn Annwn is tracking it, but I very reasonably point out that if he was using it to track me, he would have found me by now.

And...I might be starting to trust her, but there's a small, scared part of me that is afraid she'll take the magical coin and leave without me. She must see the fear on my face, because she doesn't press me.

It will take most of the three days to get everything in order with her ship. From what I understand, even with the exit spell, we won't entirely know where it will send us. In our realm, yes, but that could be anywhere.

For two nights, I listen to Maura detail her plans. How she's outfitting the ship with plenty of food in case we're nowhere near land. How she's allowing the crew short trips inland to work some of their frustrations off. How Daichi and Cai are keeping things in line in her absence.

Most importantly, she updates me on Bowen's actions. Apparently his trip to visit the monarch was successful, and he was granted permission to hunt. There's fear in Maura's voice when she describes how methodically he is moving through the square. It appears he's staying in The Bawdy Banquet, which is probably the only reason she hasn't pulled me out of here before now. Even so, the trip to the docks and out to the ship will be harrowing.

I care about the danger. Really, I do. But no matter how nice this room is, there's only so much entertainment to be had. I am bored out of my fucking mind. Maura tries to keep me entertained with books and puzzles, but I'm not a creature meant for stillness. It's only the threat of death that keeps me from giving in to my more chaotic impulses and slipping out to explore the island.

When Maura comes back around lunchtime on the third day, I'm about ready to climb the walls.

She shuts the door and slumps against it. "Well, that took longer than I thought it would, but the crew is now officially back on *The Kelpie*, so all we need is the exit spell, and we can get the fuck out of here."

Knowing we are getting things in place to escape without me getting murdered should make me happy, but now that there's nothing else to focus on, all I can think of is the future.

The subject we danced around for the past three days. "Maura... I want to know why you didn't show up at our meeting place like you promised. I understand why you didn't sail into the harbor...but you didn't come at all."

She drags her hand over her face and nods. "Seiko is bringing up lunch and drinks. Let me clean up a little bit, and then we'll talk. Actually talk."

I search her expression for some kind of trickery, but all I see is exhaustion. The past couple of days have taken their toll on me too. And though part of me wants to push this right now, what difference does a few minutes make? "Okay."

I watch her strip out of her jacket and toe off her boots. She sinks onto the bed and sighs. The silence between us has just begun to get awkward when someone knocks on the door, a quick rap that makes us both tense.

I nod at Maura and move to the corner of the room so I can't easily be seen from the door. She's been very careful to keep me out of sight from both patrons and the owner. From what she recounted of her second interaction with the hunter, it doesn't seem like anyone on this island is a fan of the Cŵn Annwn. But I can't imagine Atlantis is all that different from other places. Gold is gold is gold, no matter what currency. A lot of people will compromise their personal feelings for money.

The food is delivered quickly, a quiet word exchanged and the tray passed over. Then we're alone again.

Maura places the tray on the small table, and we each take a seat. All the awkwardness from our previous silence is back. It presses against my skin, a weight I cannot escape. I want to believe things will be okay. I want to believe she's changed her mind. But I'm not entirely certain I can trust her.

"Do you know what got me through those first few years after your father chased me out of Ashye?"

It seems like a trick question, if not for the thread of vulnerability in her voice. The temptation to make a quip about her living the pirate life dies behind my lips. "Please tell me."

"You." Maura won't quite meet my gaze. "You were all I could think of while I was working my way up the ranks of the crew I fell in with. Of getting back to you. Of taking you away from the palace where you seemed so miserable."

"I was miserable." I found ways to distract myself from that misery, but it accompanied me every day of my life under my father's thumb.

Maura fiddles with the fork in front of her. "When I became

captain, the first thing I did was try to come for you. You know how that went."

"You almost died," I whisper.

"Yeah." She gives a bare smile. "So I figured I just needed a better crew to try again. It took years to build the crew I wanted to run with. But in that time, the memory of you started to change. I never stopped loving you, Jules. That's not what I mean. But the older I got it, the more the realities of the world started to wear me down."

I understand. I don't want to know or give her any ammunition in regards to being right to send me home, but I understand the way the world can diminish a memory. "Those times with you started to feel like a dream."

"Yes, exactly that." She sits back with a huff. "Money makes the world go 'round. It didn't matter how many ships I hunted or what spoils I was able to barter because I could never get enough money to replace the life I would be asking you to leave if you ran away with me."

"But you didn't ask me. You never tried to come back again."

She nods. "Rumors reached me, even at sea. I heard about how you'd grown into the darling of the court. That you had countless lovers and paramours, and that you were always found in the latest fashion, draped in jewels from head to toe."

I stare in disbelief. "We talked about this when we were teenagers. Surviving court is its own kind of battlefield. I did what I had to, and in the end, even that wasn't enough for my father. It took me a long time to realize nothing I ever do will be good enough."

"I remember what we talked about. But so much had changed for me, and I couldn't comprehend a reality where so much hadn't changed for you as well." She shakes her head sharply. "I was wrong, Jules. I was wrong about it all, but seeing you again after all these years fucked with my head something fierce. Seeing you in danger. All I could think of was that I needed to get you safe, and in my head, safety meant sending you home."

I hate that I understand. But I do. Maybe if we had seen each other more during those important years when we transitioned from children into adults. Maybe if we had spoken, even a little bit.

Either way, we can't change the past. We can only change the future.

Right now, I have to decide if I'm willing to stay angry or if, instead, I can look to the future too. In the end, it really depends on Maura and what she says next. "And now?"

"Now?" She pushes to her feet and comes around the small table, then sinks to her knees before me. I've never seen her look like this, her expression fully open and hiding nothing. Not her guilt over how things fell out. Not her frustration over the past couple of days. And not her love for me. Maura takes my hands slowly, almost as if she expects me to jerk them away. When I don't, she smiles. "Now, Jules, I just want *you*. We have so much lost time to make up for. I can't give you the life you're accustomed to, but—"

"If I wanted that life, I would've married that old monarch in the north." I grip her hands tightly. "All I want—all I've ever wanted—is you. Just you, Maura. You when you were a penniless orphan. You when you had just joined your first crew. You as pirate captain of *The Kelpie*. It doesn't matter to me as long as we're together."

"It won't be easy."

"Life never is. But if I have you, it's worth it. Don't you feel the same?"

Maura's smile goes a little wobbly. "Yeah, Jules. I feel the same." She takes a deep breath. "I love you. Some days, it feels like I spent my entire life loving you."

It's hard to speak past the thickness in my throat, but I manage. "I love you, too."

A soft knock on the door breaks the moment. Maura frowns and rises to her feet. "That shouldn't be Seiko." She draws one of her longer daggers and holds it point down close to her thigh. She presses a single finger to her lips, but I don't need her to tell me to be quiet.

I scoot my chair back just a little bit, so I won't be immediately visible when she cracks open the door. Maura takes a visible breath, straightens her spine, and opens it.

The only warning I get is a muffled curse from her. Then she's shoved back by a bigger body, and the door's thrown open. I stare at the man revealed there. He's tall, and fearsome, and wearing a distinctive crimson cloak. Just like the Cŵn Annwn back in my father's court.

"Oh, no."

Maura springs forward, her knife raised. I haven't seen her fight properly in a very long time, but she was fierce even when we were children.

She's no match for him.

He leans back just enough to miss her swipe, and he catches her elbow before she can recover, then pulls some nasty-looking move that makes her fingers splay open and the knife fall to the ground. "That's enough of that." His voice is low and rough. This is no toothless hunter, easily distracted by the charms of others. I would never have dared steal from *him*.

He kicks the door shut behind him. Maura tries to attack again, and this time he doesn't even bother to dodge; he just plants a hand in the center of her chest and shoves her. She stumbles back and lands on the bed.

He points a blunt finger at her. "Stay down, or next time I really will hurt you."

"If you want to kill her, you have to go through me." She sits up and shoves her hair back from her face.

"Whether anyone gets hurt relies entirely on you."

I jolt a little when I realize he's talking to me, not Maura. "What are you talking about?"

He casts a long look at her and then takes a step back so he can keep both of us in his field of vision. "First, you will give back what you stole."

"Who says she stole anything?"

I sigh. "I think we may be past that." I grab my bag off the floor and feel around inside it until I come up with the piece of eight I lifted from the last Cŵn Annwn. I hold it up. "Is this what you've come all this way looking for?"

"It's a start." He holds out one of those big hands expectantly. I almost throw it right out the window, but I'm not entirely certain he would leave us alone to go chase it. And pulling a shitty move like that will exterminate whatever little goodwill we have from him. It can't be much, but he hasn't killed me yet. That's something.

I hope.

I swallow hard. "And the rest?"

"You have crossed the Cŵn Annwn. Normally that is a death sentence. However, in this scenario, because you came to Atlantis, which sits between realms, there's a little leeway. As a result, you will now be offered a choice."

"No," Maura whispers.

If this choice put that tone in her voice, I'm not going to like it. But I don't see a way out of this in our current position. "What choice?"

"The same choice we offer all those who end up in our territory." He draws himself up, suddenly seeming much larger than he was before. "You may join my crew. Or you die."

18

MAURA

I can't beat Bowen. Maybe it would be different on the open seas, with water all around me. But in this tight room, with his superior strength and reach? I can't even get close enough to strike. And the bastard is so damn fast. He hasn't even bothered to use his magic...

Then again, neither have I.

I look over at Juliette, but she's staring at the Cŵn Annwn. There's no way to signal that she should run the second I strike, so I just have to hope she understands in the moment.

The whole time we've been in Atlantis, I've kept my magic coiled tight around me. We're on land, for one. And I've learned the hard way over the years that it's best not to telegraph your strengths and weaknesses in a new place. You never know when you're going to have to fight for your life.

Like right now.

When I was a child, I had to focus my magic with my hands, but these days all takes is a single breath to direct my intention. As I told Juliette when we were teenagers, most living beings have some level of water inside them. Bowen is no different. He's human—or whatever the equivalent is in his realm.

I reach out with my mind, quick as a striking mermaid, and grab every single drop of water in his body. He makes a strangled sound and goes tense. It's all the opportunity we need. "Run, Juliette," I grit out. "I can't hold him long." Even now, he's fighting my magical grip. I've never had someone do this before; normally, they're so freaked out to be held in place, they freeze.

Not Bowen. He's eerily calm as he tracks me with those dark eyes. In fact—

Juliette grabs my arm and yanks me forward just as the metal plate formerly containing our food goes spinning through the air with enough strength to embed itself in the wall behind me.

If I hadn't moved, he would've taken my head.

Holy shit, he's telekinetic. *We're not getting out of this.* But even as I think it, I'm readying myself to fight. I've always battled hard for survival, but what is survival compared to hope? I desperately want the future the Juliette and I spoke about just a little while ago. If this bastard kills her or takes her into his crew and sails away with her, I'll never see her again.

I clench my fist and jerk it toward me, attempting to yank every drop of water from his body. "Let's see you survive this, fucker."

The veins stand out in Bowen's thick neck, and his complexion goes dark and mottled. He's...fighting me? I can feel the water trying to respond to my command, but somehow he's keeping it in place through the sheer force of his telekinetic powers. This guy is a monster.

Sweat breaks out along my hairline, and my body starts to shake. "Juliette, *run.*"

Of course she doesn't. Instead, she rushes forward. She scoops up my fallen dagger in a practiced move and lunges for Bowen.

It all happens so fast. He snaps my hold and jerks a hand up in time to catch her around the throat. I don't even have time to yell before he pins her to the wall and yanks the dagger out of her hands. "That is *enough*." He hardly sounds winded, when my body is shaking like a leaf. It's easier to control the water of the sea than it is to find and control water in a body. My failure might just mean our deaths.

Bowen points his stolen dagger at me. "If you move an inch, I will crush her throat."

My mind races, coming up with and discarding dozens of plans in the span of a heartbeat. All of them are too risky to Juliette. "Let her go." I hate how much my voice shakes, but I can't help it. "Take the piece of eight back. We'll return to our realm, and we can all pretend this never happened. It was a mistake. We never meant to come here."

"Most people never intend to end up in Threshold, either. Intentions don't matter. Results do." He sounds almost bored as he says it, as if these are words he's recited countless times before and will recite countless times in the future. The very thought is horrifying.

I open my mouth to say something. I don't know what, though, because nothing seems likely to convince him to let us go. I never get a chance.

A wave of a magic rolls through the room with the force of a tsunami. All three of us flinch, and then the feeling hits me. It's hot and sizzling, a physical sensation coursing through my body like the best kind of foreplay. I stagger. In the back of my mind, something is screaming to use this to my advantage, but all I can do is think of sex. There's a bed right behind me, after all. And Juliette is *right there*. I don't have much use for Bowen... Wait, what am I saying?

He can watch.

What the fuck? No. I fist my hands at my side to prevent myself from doing something part of me knows I'll regret. The rest of me is pretty on board with anything that gets Juliette's hands on my body and mouths on my skin. "What the fuck is happening?" I manage to grind out.

"Siren." Bowen sounds just as strangled as I do, and I watch him stroke Juliette's neck with his thumb. Almost as if he can't help himself.

"Maybe we could..." Juliette writhes against the wall, her hips obviously seeking friction. "Just a little. "

Bowen jerks back from her as if she's burned him. He gives me a scorching look. "This isn't over." And then he bolts from the room.

"Oh good. It's just the two of us. I prefer it that way." Juliette starts to work her dress over her head.

The last of my hesitation leaves the room with the Cŵn Annwn. How can I resist how good I already feel, when Juliette is stripped to the skin in front of me? I don't need magic to want her like this.

There's something we need to do...somewhere we need to go...

The magic washes it all away. There's only the throbbing between my thighs and the weightiness of my tongue. I need to taste her, and I need to do it now. I scramble out of my clothes, rushing to meet her. We clash in a tangle of questing hands and wanton mouths.

It always feels good to touch Juliette, to taste her. But it's on another level entirely right now. Every sensation is heightened. She drags a single finger down the curve of my breast, and I nearly orgasm on the spot. "More."

"Now who's begging?" She starts to go to her knees, but I'm having none of that. I refuse to allow any more distance between us than absolutely necessary. I tumble us back onto the bed and flip her beneath me. Or at least I try. Juliette uses the momentum to flip us back, with her ending up on top. She grins down at me, particularly proud of herself.

Then her mouth is on mine and time ceases to have meaning. There's only her hands on my body and her skin sliding against mine. Magic drives us, escalating our pleasure and drowning out all else. My worries, my fears, even my plans are all washed away as we make each other come again and again and again.

19

JULIETTE

"**G**et up, Juliette. We have to go."

I slowly open my eyes and blink a few times until the room comes into focus. It's not the only thing that becomes clear. Holy crap, that really just happened. We just went from a fight for our lives into a fuckfest beyond my wildest dreams. Though it could've been so much worse if Bowen had stayed. I shudder. If that's the power of sirens, I think I understand why the monarch doesn't want them on this island.

"Juliette." Maura's already dressed, her sword belted around her waist. She looks like she wants to shake me and is barely restraining herself.

It takes so much more energy than it should to sit up and move to the edge of the bed. It's even harder to focus. What had she said? *We have to go.* "Is the exit spell ready?"

"Yes. Seiko gave it to me just now, but we have bigger problems. Or maybe an opportunity, depending on how you look at it." She tosses my dress to me and waits until I put it on to continue. "There's something going on in the square, and the monarch's people are blocking access to the docks."

Fear slices through me, dissipating the last of the relaxation that came from stellar sex. The Cŵn Annwn knows where we are now. If we can't reach the docks, how are we supposed to exit the island? I slide my hand into my pocket, and the fear gets worse. In the scuffle, I never did give the Cŵn Annwn back the piece of eight I stole.

"He's never going to stop coming."

"I've been running for half my life." Maura grins, fierce and feral. "Give me an entire realm of seas that I know like the back of my hand, and he'll never find us. We just have to get off this fucking island."

It strikes me that this is a part of Maura I haven't seen in a decade, the part that revels in the chase as much as the hunt. If I go with her, if I join her crew, this will be my life. Hunting and fleeing in turn.

A kernel of excitement takes root in my belly. "How are we going to do that?"

"Come now, Juliette. Have a little faith. There's a reason your father hasn't caught me yet. I like to plan for every eventuality. My crew knows what to do, but we have to move now." She's almost giddy as she speaks, and I am forcibly reminded of how she was when we were younger. Ruthless and cunning, yes, but also a thrill seeker like none other.

Apparently she hasn't outgrown it, and that pleases me to an unholy degree despite our circumstances. If we can live through this, I think we're going to have a lot of fun. "Okay, I'm moving." I yank on my shoes and smooth down my hair as much as possible. It wouldn't pass even a cursory glance from my father or his court, but no one on this island cares that I've been fucking my girlfriend. The freedom makes me absolutely giddy despite the danger we're currently in.

Maura leads the way down the back staircase that we came up when we first arrived at the inn. Somehow, I'm not even remotely surprised to see Seiko lounging against the doorway.

She raises her brows at us. "It's not safe to be out and about right now."

"We know. That's why it's time for us to leave." Maura nods to her. "Thank you for the hospitality and for the exit spell— even if you did charge me through the nose for both."

"Business is business, lovely." She moves out of the way. "Don't be a stranger."

"Honestly, Seiko, if I ever see you again, it will be because something has gone terribly wrong."

She bursts out laughing. "Fair enough. Happy travels. "

As I begin to follow Maura past Seiko, I pause. "Please make sure the Cŵn Annwn gets this."

She looks at the piece of eight in my palm, and her eyes go wide. "That explains a few things."

Part of me wants to elaborate, but the truth is that I don't know this woman, and I don't really know where her allegiance lies. But I think she wants the hunter gone as much as anyone, so she'll pass it on. I drop it into her hand and

follow Maura through the door to the outside. Somewhere close, I can hear raised voices, but Maura leads me away from them and toward a small footpath through the trees that I hadn't noticed before.

She must see my confusion, because she laughs. "Come now, Jules. You don't think I spent all those hours over the past two days tracking down Daichi, do you? First lesson of piracy— always have half a dozen exit routes in place for when shit goes sideways. Because if there's one rule of the world, it's that shit will *always* go sideways."

"I'm learning so much already." And I am. She hasn't lost that reckless part of her, after all. Apparently it just comes out when danger is at its highest.

"Do not, under any circumstances, leave the path. It's barely safe as it is, so step where I step and move where I move."

"Yes, ma'am."

She turns just enough to give me a sharp look. "None of that."

Her excitement is infecting me as well. I feel downright giddy. "None of what?"

"You know exactly what." She draws her dagger and slows. "From how you handled yourself in the inn, you know how to use one of these."

Surprise almost causes me to make a smartass quip, but the gravity of the situation quickly stifles that. "Yes, I bullied the weapons master into training me. He refused to show me how to use a sword, but even he had to agree that a knife is great self-defense if my guard fails for some reason."

"That's solid reasoning, but the first thing we're going to do when we get out of here is teach you how to use a sword."

I don't know what to feel right now. Giddy and delighted that the future I always wanted has a solid chance of coming to fruition. Terrified that everything I've ever desired is now within my grasp but I've never been in more danger than I am in this moment. The Cŵn Annwn could take everything from me. My life, yes, but more importantly, my future with Maura. A future filled with freedom and love.

I wrap my fingers around the hilt of the dagger. I'm not violent by nature, but it feels like I've never had something to fight for until this moment. I will not let the Cŵn Annwn get between us and our escape.

When we were escorted to the court, I will admit I felt a measure of curiosity about the forest. Like so many other things on the island, it's filled with both the familiar and the strange; there are things here that I will never get a chance to see again, not as long as I live. The danger's real enough that I don't think I would've entered the cover of the trees, but the temptation was there all the same.

It's not there anymore.

The greenery presses against the path like long leafy

fingers. No matter how small I try to make myself, they brush against my skin and tangle with my skirts. At first, it's almost a teasing touch. So light, I barely notice it. But, like a yipping puppy, it's almost as if my determination to ignore it incites the trees instead. Which is ridiculous. There are trees, for gods' sake.

But...magical trees *do* exist in my realm, too.

I catch a glimpse of pale blue in the distance. It's such a surprising color that I slow. "Did you see that?"

"Do I need to revisit the conversation in which all the dangers of this place were detailed out for you?" Maura grabs my wrist. "Don't slow down, Jules. It's not safe, and we don't have time to linger even if it were."

She doesn't release me through the rest of the trip through the forest. In fact, she practically drags me up the last hill, her grip so tight, it almost hurts. I'm not about to complain, though. Not when the blue lights in the forest start appearing with more regularity. By the time we clear the trees, one flares to life close enough to the path that I think I see a face in its blue depths. I shudder. As much as I enjoy the adventure of this place, Maura really is right about the dangers.

We exit the forest and walk out onto a perfectly manicured field. It's so strange that I almost miss a step. "What is this place?"

"Another entrance."

I'm about to ask what Maura means by that when I see the large metal contraption. Though *contraption* may not be the right word; it's a large gray platform that stands at waist height, with an equally gray set of stairs leading from the ground up to it. I frown. "A portal?"

"I don't think so." Maura charges past it. She doesn't let me pause to linger, even when bright colored lights flicker to life on a square pad near the staircase. I've never seen anything like it, and I don't know if that frightens or excites me. Maybe both.

We leave the strange platform behind as we move toward the cliff face overlooking the water, and then I have bigger things to worry about.

"There's a path that leads down to the water from here, but it's pretty treacherous. I'll go first. Same rules as before—you step where I step and move where I move. Do you understand, Jules?"

I take a few steps closer to the cliff's edge and look over. Vertigo hits me hard enough that I have to focus on planting my feet and not tipping right over the edge. We must've climbed higher than I realized, because the water is a long... long...way down. Far below, the waves crash against rocks that look sharp and deadly and ready to catch someone in their fatal embrace. "There isn't room for a ship to get close here. Not without risking hull damage."

"I know." Maura pats herself down, seemingly checking to make sure everything is fastened in place. "We'll have to swim."

"*Swim?*"

"Yes." Maura takes my shoulders. "*The Kelpie* is sailing north right now along the shore of the island. We just have to get down to the water, Jules. My magic will propel us to the ship. I won't let you drown. I promise."

There are so many things that can go wrong. I could fall, and even Maura's water magic wouldn't be able to save me from those rocks. *Maura* could fall. My chest tightens at the thought of her dying. I shake my head sharply. "No. It's too dangerous. There has to be another way."

"There is no other way."

The wind whips Maura's blonde hair around her face. It was calm a few seconds ago, but now I can taste the storm coming. Oh gods, we really are running out of time. The longer we stand here arguing, the worse it's going to be. Either I trust her, or I don't. I swallow hard. "Okay. Let's go."

"Remember—follow me exactly." Maura starts down the

narrow path. It looked harrowing before, but seeing exactly how little room there is for error makes my stomach drop. I'm graceful enough when I need to be, but I don't have much experience with scaling cliff walls. I'm not a fucking goat.

My skin prickles and I shiver. This wind really is...

Except it's not the wind my instincts are trying to warn me about. I hear the crunch of boots on rock and spin around to see the Cŵn Annwn standing a few feet away. He looks like shit, the lines around his mouth deeper than they were just a few hours ago. There was no kindness on his expression the last time we met, but I didn't realize until this moment that he wasn't angry when we fought in the inn room.

He's angry now.

"Choose, Princess Juliette of Skoiya. I will not ask you again."

Choose. Death, or a life that may as well be death. I tighten my grip on the dagger. Even if I choose now, there's nothing to stop him from killing Maura. She's helpless, too far down the cliff path to attack him and not nearly far enough to make the fall to the water below safely.

It's up to me to protect her.

I don't give myself time to think. That's the first lesson my weapons master taught me; if you're thinking, you telegraph your intentions to your opponent. My body moves on impulse, my arm whipping out as I release the dagger. It's not meant for throwing; it's a little too long and not weighted properly. It's still my best chance.

Or at least that's what I think until the hunter flings out his hand and a wave of power hits me like a runaway carriage. I barely have a chance to remember that he's telekinetic and dastardly strong before I'm flung backward.

Over the cliff's edge.

20

MAURA

I hear a scream and look up in time to see Juliette fly over the edge of the cliff above me. It's not an accidental fall; she is too far away from the edge for that to make sense. No, she was pushed. The understanding hits me in the span of a heartbeat. I don't stop to think. There's no time.

I leap from the cliff with every bit of strength I have and collide with Juliette midair. She still screaming. I clutch her to me and throw out a hand in the direction of the water below us. I'm still so damn tired from the fight with the Cŵn Annwn earlier, but I put every bit of strength I have into dragging the ocean up to meet us. It doesn't have to be far, just deep enough that we won't die on the rocks below.

It feels like trying to fight gravity.

We're falling too fast. It's rising too slow. Another beat, maybe two, and we will hit the rocks. That will be the end of us.

No.

I fucking *refuse.*

My scream joins Juliette's, picking up where hers starts to falter. Rage. All I feel is rage. At all the years I missed spending in her presence. At her father and my pride for keeping us apart. At the damned Cŵn Annwn for ruining the future I want so desperately.

The ocean surges.

It rises to meet us, and we hit hard enough that I wonder if there was any point in this at all. It hurts. *Everything* hurts. The water closes over our heads, and we sink. Now is the time to move, to swim to the surface and figure out exactly how long we need to survive before *The Kelpie* comes to scoop us up.

My arms and legs aren't responding to my brain's commands to move. My lungs aren't responding either. My mind shrieks at me to move, to swim, to do *something* to keep us from drowning. Nothing happens. It's as if I'm trapped in a body that's already dead.

An arm clamps around my waist, and then I'm being dragged through the water. Up and up and up. The pressure is so intense that I almost open my mouth and let the sea in. I can't do that. I can't give up now, not when I'm so close to the surface once more.

We break through the surface with a gasp. My rescuer turns me over onto my back and bands an arm beneath my breasts. It takes several long seconds before my exhausted mind registers the soft gasping breaths as belonging to Juliette.

She saved me.

"Damned...Cŵn Annwn... I'll...kill him." She drags me to a low rock and manages to cling to the edge of it. "My weapons master...might've been right about my impulsiveness. Also, holy shit, adrenaline is a wild drug."

I try to speak but only end up hacking. It takes several long minutes to spew out water that apparently slipped past my lips and into my lungs. I want to help, but all I can do is submit as Juliette turns my head to the side so I don't choke. I can't do anything but fight not to drown now that she's saved me.

"A few more minutes." She sounds as exhausted as I feel, but she makes no move to wrestle me onto the little rock. "Better that he thinks we're dead."

It takes far too long for her meaning to penetrate. He. Bowen. That must be whom she's talking about. I cough a little more. "Bowen pushed you?"

"He's telekinetic," Juliette reminds me. She has to pause to adjust her grip on both me and the rock. Each wave that comes in threatens to dislodge us. "I threw the dagger, and he defended in a more robust way than I expected. I don't know if he meant to throw me."

She's giving him a lot more grace than I want to in this moment.

"Maura. I really need you to be okay."

I have to wait my way through another coughing fit before I can respond. "I'll be fine. I just need a little bit of time." I really hope I'm not lying.

"Yeah, about that. I think the tide's coming in." Her voice is fainter than it was before. We're both too exhausted to survive much longer. Juliette clutches me tighter to her. "And, um, I think the mermaids aren't only on the south side of the island."

Somehow, there's energy left in my body. Fear has a way of expanding limits, and there's no fear like being in mermaid-infested water without any defenses. I manage to move my arms and legs enough to turn and look where Juliette is focused.

They're coming.

There are multiple types of mermaid in our realm alone. The deep-water ones who only rise to the surface during their breeding season. The poisonous ones who hunt tropical waters around certain currents. And the ones like those streaming toward us. The shallow-water hunters. Those who wait until their prey can see land and think safety is within reach. I swear they feed on despair as much as they do on flesh and blood.

I don't see a way out of this. Even *The Kelpie* sometimes has problems with mermaids, and that's a full-size ship with a crew trained in sea battle. Right now, I'm drained of all but the last dregs of my power. Juliette may be formidable in a number of ways, but not even she can battle a horde of mermaids intent on the hunt.

In a burst of strength, she manages to drag us both onto the little rock. It's less than nothing when it comes to defense, but at least we aren't in the water. I drag in a rough breath. "I love you."

"Don't you fucking dare." Juliette crouches over me, her expression feral. "Don't you dare give up hope. We're not dead yet."

No, we're not dead yet, but the mermaids are almost to us, so that will change quickly. "Juliette—"

"There!" She points. "*The Kelpie* is right *there!*"

I manage to twist enough to look south. Sure enough, *The Kelpie* is racing toward us, hugging the coastline as close as can be. Too far. It's still too damn far away. Even with full sails, which would be a suicidal move if not for all the elementals on my crew, they'll never reach us in time. Not to mention the rocks will keep them from scooping us right up.

"Juliette. Jules. I'm sorry. I—"

The mermaids reach us. They shriek in bloodthirsty delight as they spiral around our rock. It's a terrifying experience, but what comes next will be worse. As if they can read my fear, the mermaids dive deep.

"Get down," I rasp. "They're coming."

Julia crouches over me, fully ignoring my command. Protecting me. Gods, I love this woman. I don't deserve her. *We* don't deserve this end.

Another set of screeches as the mermaids breach the surface. One flies directly over us, its outstretched claws missing Juliette by a hair. I try to pull her more on top of me, to plaster us to the surface of the rock, but she easily pushes my hands away.

The next mermaid doesn't miss. It adjusted its trajectory and is going to sweep us right off the rock. I move in a surge of strength to yank Juliette down to me. It's not enough, but at least we won't get separated in the impact. Hopefully.

Again, she slips out of my grasp. Juliette strikes with the dagger, cutting into the mermaid's outstretched hand. It shrieks in pain and flops back into the water. A beat. Two. Then the others swarm their injured companion and the waters turn frothing and red.

"What's going on?"

"Cannibals," I gasp. "Any injury draws them."

She narrows her eyes. "We can do this. I just need to keep cutting them."

No, we can't. There are too many. Even now, most of them are breaking away from the feast to dive again. "Get down."

"You've saved me enough, Maura. I'm going to save you this time." She adjusts her grip on the dagger. I want to tell her this is impossible, to tell her I love her again. I don't get a chance before the mermaids attack again.

Again, Jules strikes out, slicing at them again and again. One gets it's claws into her hair and nearly drags her over the edge before she cuts it. Around us, the water turns red with blood.

"*The Kelpie* is almost here," she pants.

I twist to follow her gaze. She's right. The ship is close enough that I can see my crew on the deck, their arms moving rhythmically as they use the ocean wind to skim over the waves in our direction.

Almost here...but still not close enough.

We'll have to swim. I take a deep breath and scan myself internally. I don't have much magic left. I've only expended this much once before, when a hurricane came out of nowhere and nearly killed everyone on my ship. It took every single one of us to get through that, and at the end of it, me and most of my crew were so exhausted that we could've slept for days. I don't know what happens if I use the last of my magic reserves. I don't know if I'll pass out...or if I'll die.

But if I don't try, we will both definitely die.

"Help me up."

Juliette hesitates, but there's no time. She curses and loops an arm around my waist. We stagger to our feet and turn to survey *The Kelpie*. It's so close. I try to weigh the distance, but my brain feels fuzzy. I don't have to get us all the way there; I just need to get close enough for the crew to gather us up.

I don't know if I can do it.

I don't have a choice.

"Whatever you do, don't let go of me." I want to be strong enough to save Juliette, but she's going to have to be strong enough for both of us.

"Okay."

The mermaids are still attacking each other as much as they're aiming for us. Getting through the frenzy is going to require pure luck. Juliette hooks her hands into my belt. I do my best to cling to her as well. She gives me one brief, desperate kiss. "We're going to live."

You will. I move us to the edge of the rock and tip us into the water. In a perfect world, I would dive forward and build up momentum on my own that I could supplement with my magic. That's not an option right now. I dig deep and pull the dregs of my magic to me. It hurts. Holy fuck, it hurts. The magic burrows into me, feeling like it's sucking every bit of vitality from my very bones. I ignore the pain; it's only temporary, after all, and when this is through, I can rest for good.

Juliette clings to me as I propel us through the water. I'm

distantly aware of the screeching of mermaids but somehow none of them makes contact. Black dances across my vision. I hope we're close enough to *The Kelpie* to get help, because I have nothing left.

The whole world goes dark.

21

JULIETTE

It takes me far too long to realize Maura has gone limp in my arms. When the water surges around us and lifts us into the air, at first I think she's responsible. It's not until we're gently deposited on the deck of *The Kelpie* that I realize she's passed out. "Maura!"

Hands grab my shoulders and pull me away from Maura's limp body. I fight them, but I'm pathetically weak right now. It's only when I'm shoved back and Daichi appears before me that I realize he was the one holding me.

His expression is drawn. "Give the healer space. He'll take care of her, but he can't do that if you're in the way."

My heart climbs into my throat as a boy who looks far too young crouches next to Maura. He holds a hand over her chest and closes his eyes. I tense, searching the space between his hand and her chest for some kind of indication of the magic working. There's nothing. "She has to be okay," I say.

"She's the captain. Of course she'll be okay." Daichi might be more believable if the statement didn't come out more like a question. "Just give it time."

That's the problem; I'm not sure we have time. "The Cŵn

Annwn. He was on the cliffs. If he comes after us—"

"He won't get a chance. The exit spell is in place." Cai speaks from zir place at the helm. "We're getting the fuck out of here." Ze barks commands at the air mages wielding their powers to keep the sales tight and the ship skimming over the surface of the sea. The ship turns for open water, far faster than I've ever seen a ship maneuver.

Maybe we really will escape.

That's good, but my priority right now is Maura.

The healer sits back on his heels and emits a string of curses, the likes I've never heard before. I must be delirious because I have the most ridiculous urge to write them down so I won't forget them. He turns and looks at me and Daichi. "Burnout."

Daichi curses.

I look between them, the heaviness in my chest getting worse. "What does that mean?" Obviously I know magical burnout is fatal, but that can't be what they're talking about. Maura cannot die. I won't allow it.

The healer shrugs, but his nonchalance is ruined by the sick expression on his face. "There's nothing I can do. Either she'll recover on her own, or..."

"No. Do not say 'or' to me. She's going to recover." My voice sounds more forceful than it ever has in my life. I hate the way it looks like he's already mourning the loss of Maura. Fuck that. She's going to live.

"Daichi, take the captain and Juliette to her cabin. Things are going to get rough."

I follow Cai's gaze to the sky darkening in front of us. The clouds look green and almost yellow in places. We don't see many storms like that in Ashye, but people still talk about the hurricane that came through the fall after I was born. From the stories, the clouds looked a lot like the ones in front of us.

"That's a ship killer," I say.

"Not for us." Daichi rises and walks over to where Maura lies. He scoops her up gently and starts for the captain's quarters. The wind whips at my hair and clothes. All around me, the crew members are tying themselves off with determined looks on their faces. Maybe this isn't a ship killer for *The Kelpie*, but that doesn't mean it's not dangerous.

I scramble to my feet and follow Daichi. It's quieter inside the captain's quarters, but all that means is there's nothing to distract me from Maura. Daichi sets her on the bed and turns to me. "They need me out there." He hesitates, clearly torn. "Can you stay here and keep her safe?"

"Yes, of course." As if I would be anywhere but at her side. I barely wait for him to move before I take a place next to her. The bed swings wildly, but it's still moving less wildly than the ship itself. We climb and fall what feel like mountains. I knew things could get bad, but knowing something in theory and experiencing it firsthand are two extremely different things.

There's nothing for me to do except ensure Maura stays safe while we escape Atlantis. I climb more fully onto the bed and gather her into my arms. She's still breathing, at least for now. I can't help pressing my hand to her chest and measuring each inhale and exhale.

"I need you to be okay. You got us to the ship. You've saved me half a dozen times in the past couple of days. We didn't get this far for you to die now." My voice is ragged, and my throat feels like I swallowed embers. "We have a future, Maura. The whole fucking world has tried to stand between us, but we finally have a future. I need you to be there with me. I don't think I can do it alone." My voice breaks. It wasn't supposed to be like this. "This is all my fault. None of this would've happened if I hadn't stolen the piece of eight and then triggered the entrance to Atlantis. I am so, so fucking sorry."

"Always so dramatic."

For a second, I think I'm imagining things. But then Maura

moves in my arms, and her eyes flutter open. She smiles faintly. "We made it."

"Yeah, we got here because of you. We're safe now."

The ship chooses that moment to hit a dip that sends us swinging sharply; my stomach threatens to rebel.

Maura frowns. "Doesn't feel safe."

She tries to sit up, but I push her down onto her back. It's frighteningly easy. "Oh, no, you don't. You almost died. Cai has things well in hand, and ze will get us through. Trust your crew. I do."

Almost as if my words contain magic, the intense seesawing of the ship evens out. I can still feel us skimming the tops of waves, but it's almost as if the storm disappeared in an instant. Maybe we're in the eye of the storm?

A cheer goes up on the other side of the captain's door. I barely have a moment to wonder what's going on when the door's thrown open and Daichi bursts in. He skids to a stop. His eyes go wide at the sight of Maura awake. A giant grin appears on his face. "You're okay, Captain."

"Right as rain." Maura sounds like death warmed over, but she's speaking, and it's the most beautiful thing I've ever heard.

His grin widens. "Then I think you're going to want to see this."

I expect him to carry her, but he just steps back and watches as she struggles to her feet. I'm not having any of that. I duck under her arm, ignoring her grumbling, and don't comment on just how much weight I'm taking from her. We stagger out of the captain's quarters and into bright sunlight.

Cai gives us a grin just as wide as Daichi's. "We missed you, Captain." Like the rest of the crew I can see, ze is soaked to the bone, zir clothes plastered to zir body.

"I'm here now." Maura's voice is even raspier than mine. She leans more heavily on me. "Update me."

"The exit spell seems to have worked." Cai points to something in the distance. "I can't be entirely sure until we're closer, but I think that's Emerald Island. The water there looks the same as the one we're currently sailing through."

We're back.

Relief hits me hard enough to buckle my knees, quickly followed by dread. We've made so many promises to each other, but we did it in a place out of both time and space. Will those promises hold up now that we're back in our own realm?

Maura inhales deeply. "We have enough supplies to see us through several weeks. Daichi, set course for Etra."

She speaks so decisively, I almost give in to the temptation not to question it. But I can't seem to help myself. "Why there?"

"It's as good a place as any." Maura lifts her chin and closes her eyes. "I think the threat of the Cŵn Annwn should be past. He has the stolen piece of eight, and we're back in our own realm, beyond their territory in Threshold. But there's no reason to be reckless. We'll stay on the move." She opens her eyes and smiles. "I have so much to show you. "

Hope sprouts wings in my chest and takes flight. I try for a smile, but I feel shaky around the edges. "Does that mean you're not shoving me in the nearest carriage and sending me back to Ashye?"

Maura turns to me and cups my face in her hands. She's shaking just a little, and I can't tell if it's emotion or the fact she just almost died. She presses a gentle kiss to my lips. "I'm yours, Jules. As long as you'll have me, I'm yours. Nothing and no one will ever come between us again. I *will* have the future with you that we promised each other. "

My throat is hot and tight. She means it. She really, really means it. "I love you so much."

"I love you, too." Maura turns to face the horizon, and we slowly move to the railing. "There's a whole wide world out there, Jules. And it's all ours."

I can't stop smiling. "Show me everything."

EPILOGUE
JULIETTE

It turns out getting intimate on a pirate ship is a lot easier said than done. Now that I'm part of the crew on The Kelpie, my days are filled to the brim with work. It's a lot more enjoyable than expected...and exhausting. But we made port last night, which means half the crew has gone ashore to engage in all sorts of fun and lecherous activities.

It also means that I have Maura all to myself.

She's in the shower now, washing off the day's exertion. It means I don't have much time. I step in front of the mirror and survey myself critically. I feel like a different person from the woman who bought this lingerie before orchestrating her own kidnapping.

But I can't deny *that* woman had exquisite taste.

The soft turquoise color looks lovely against my skin. Between the lace and the various straps of ribbon, more of me is on display than is covered. It truly is a work of art. I really hope Maura thinks so, too

In the other room, the water shuts off.

I don't know why I'm so nervous. In the months since we left Atlantis, we've spent every night in bed together. Sure, most of those nights have resulted in us collapsing together in an exhausted cuddle. But it's not as if this is the first time I've set out to seduce this woman.

I drag my fingers through my hair one last time and turn as she walks through the door into the bedroom proper. Maura is naked, her skin still damp from the shower, her hair a wet mass around her face. She goes still. "What's this?"

"What does it look like?" I wave a hand to encompass my body. "Obviously it's a seduction." My heart flutters in my throat. It is so ridiculous that I'm nervous, but I can't shake the feeling.

"A seduction." Maura slicks back her hair. "I haven't seen that number before."

She's not doing anything provocative, but I'm having a hard time drawing in a full breath. It's the look in her eyes. The tension in her body. As if she's fighting not to cross the room and drag me into her arms. Honestly, that would be preferable. I don't know when I lost my edge for seduction, but even after all this time, I still feel like a fumbling teenager with her sometimes.

I lick my lips. "It was meant to be a surprise. I had a commission done before I left Skoiya."

Maura moves to the bed and sinks onto the edge of it. She motions me closer with a single finger. All thought—what little there was left—flees my head. I cross to her and step easily between her spread thighs.

She traces the band of ribbon around my stomach, her fingernail against my skin making me shiver. Her eyes narrow in the most delicious way possible and her tone goes low and seductively dangerous. "You mean you've had this for months and I'm just now seeing it?"

"It's too special to pull out on any given night, especially with how tired we've been."

Her gaze softens. "Is it too much? You haven't complained, but—"

"It's not too much," I cut in. "I like the work. It's different than I expected, more enjoyable. It makes me feel like I have a purpose beyond being a pretty thing up on the shelf."

"You are a pretty thing." Maura tugs me closer and drags her finger down to cup the lace at the apex of my thighs. "But hardly useless." She rubs my pussy through the lace. "You're already wet. Did you get started without me?"

"Of course not." When she merely lifts her brows, I laugh a little. "Well, not this time. I was just thinking about all the things I want to do to you. And you took an extremely long shower, so give me plenty of time she come up with inspiration."

"Yeah?" She leans down and nips my belly. "Tell me."

I take her shoulders impress her back onto the bed, following her down. "I never get tired of looking at you. I'll never get over the fact that you're mine and I can touch you any time I want." I drag my fingers over her clavicle and down the center of her chest. "Can taste you any time I want." I lean down and follow the path with my mouth. Fresh from the shower, she tastes of nothing but herself. Smells of nothing but herself. Maybe one day I won't get drunk on the experience it is Maura, today's not that day.

She laces her fingers through my hair and gives a sharp tug. "You're the one decorated like a pretty present, and you expect me to resist unwrapping you."

"On the contrary. I want you to unwrap me. Ribbon by ribbon." I trace the curve of one breast and then the other. "But you're here and you're naked, and I think you'll have to forgive me for being distracted."

I suck her nipple into my mouth hard, just the way she likes it. Maura gives a sweet little moan and arches her back, offering herself up to me. I'll never get tired of one of the most fearsome pirates in all our realm, who is reputation strikes such fear into the heart of merchants, they immediately surrender when they see if her flag, rather than fight it out.

And she's all mine. She's in my bed... Our bed... naked and whimpering for what only I can give her.

But then, Maura has never been passive partner. The second I start to move to her neck, she lets loose a sexy little growl and flips us. She lands astride my stomach and gives me a mock glare. "You're supposed to be my present. Stop trying to distract me. Be a good little pirate princess and let me unwrap you to my heart's delight."

The command seems easy enough to follow, but I'm impatient and needy and being told to stay still is a torture unlike any other. Maura knows this, of course. It's why she told me to do it. I grab fistfuls of the comforter and bite my bottom lip as she traces the ribbons on my body. I won't pretend that part of me didn't anticipate this exquisite teasing, of Maura taking her time to explore every inch of my body. I hardly wish I chose a less intricate design.

At least until she presses her mouth to the bare space between the lace at the top of my stockings and the lace that covers my pussy. She's kissed me in this exact place more times than I can count, but there's something about being partially clothed that undoes me. I shiver and shake and can't decide whether I want to slam my thighs close or spread them wide for her.

She doesn't give me a chance to decide. Maura runs her hands from my calves to the back of my knees and then spreads my legs wide, exposing me completely. She makes a pleased noise and I swear I can hear my pussy getting wetter in response. Maura glances up and meets my eyes. "Do I want to know how expensive it was?"

The question catches me off guard, so I speak without thinking. "Probably not." There are parts of my new life that are still downright lavish but when you're spending all your time aboard a ship with limited space, you learn to pick and choose what you really can't live without. Even so, the price for this set was ostentatious even by princess standards.

"Thought so." She leans down and rubs her face against my lace panties. "Gods, Jules. I'll have to steal from a thousand merchant ships, because I need to see you in one of these in every color. You look like my favorite dessert." She covers me with her mouth, licking me through the lace. It's decadent and desperate, and I can't get enough.

"Maura!"

She licks around the edges of the lace and then nuzzles my panties to the side so she can kiss my pussy was nothing between us. I cry out. "More!"

"I'll give you more, Juliette. I'll give you everything." She presses two fingers into me, unerringly finding that wicked spot inside me that makes my entire body go liquid and molten. I had thought this evening might be a fun tease, but Maura is wasting no time. She winds me tighter and tighter, working my body as only she can. I try to hold out of sheer perversity, but it's no use. I scream her name as I come.

She doesn't stop.

My orgasm has barely crested when she starts winding me up again. I don't make a conscious decision to dig my hands into her damp hair, but I find them there all the same. I don't know if it's to pull her off me or to urge her to never stop. I don't have a chance to decide before I'm coming again, my heels digging into the bed and my back bowing with pleasure. Again, I scream for name.

She pauses long enough to work my panties carefully down my legs and toss them the side before she's back between my thighs. "One more, Jules. Give me one more."

As if I have a choice. I'm helpless in her hands, against the onslaught of her mouth. There's a part of me that wants to turn the tables, but I'm too busy enjoying everything she does to me. Maura is nothing if not inspired when she gets in the mood, and she's obviously in the mood tonight.

I lose track of how many times I come. It's only when I'm a weak, shaking mess that she finally shifts up my body. She kisses her way over my stomach and pauses long enough to tug the lace from my breasts in give each nipple thorough kiss, before she takes my mouth. The kiss is soft and sweet and full of so much love that I could weep.

When she finally lifts her head, she whispers, "I have something for you, too." She reaches past me and delves beneath the pillow at the top of the bed. I'm so drunk on pleasure that it takes me several long blinks before I realize what she's holding in her hand.

A ring.

Not just any ring, either. It's a silver band with a giant ruby in the center. I've never seen it before, and yet it as familiar as my own hand. "How?"

"Did you think I forgot? We've been wishing on stars since we were children, Jules. How many of those wishes you made were for a ring with a diamond as red as blood?"

I would say I had forgotten, but that would be a lie. Every stolen moment I spent with Maura is imprinted on my heart and soul. Even months later, there's a part of me that continues to be surprised to find that she feels the same. "I was bloodthirsty little winch."

Maura smiles. "I loved you then, and I love you now. I never want to leave your side again, Jules. Not until death comes for us both." She licks her lips, suddenly seeming unsure. "Will you marry me? Will you be my wife, even if it means you can never go back?"

I understand why she feels like she has to ask that question. But my answer will never change. "Yes, Maura. Yes, I'll be your wife. Yes, I'll stay by your side through high tide and low, danger and times of plenty, until death comes for us both." My throat closes a little, and I have to swallow to keep going. "I love you. I've always loved you. You have always been in it for me."

Her smile as bright as the sun and she slips the ruby onto my finger. It's a perfect fit. Of course it is. Once Maura decides on something, she leaves nothing to chance. She lifts my hand and presses a kiss to my knuckles. Right next to the ring. "I know a priest in town. They would be happy to marry us tonight." She shifts until she's on top of me, pressing me down to the mattress. "Or...we can go find them tomorrow instead."

I arch up and kiss her with everything I have. "Tomorrow will be soon enough. I have plans for you tonight, wife."

Did I think her smile as bright as the sun before? It's nothing compared to her expression now. "Say it again, Jules."

"Wife." I kiss her again. "I love you so much, wife. I'm never going to get tired of calling you that."

"I'll never get tired of hearing it."

HUNT ON DARK WATERS
SNEAK PEEK

BOWEN

Keep reading for a sneak peek of Hunt on Dark Waters!

"MERMAID OFF THE STARBOARD SIDE!"

The call brings me out of my cabin. We're not in mermaid waters, but if the sighting is correct, we have one bastard of a fight on our hands. I grab a spear from the rack, noting that my first mate, Miles, has the spelled net already in his hands.

We meet on the starboard side and I narrow my eyes against the glare of the sun on the choppy water. How the lookout saw anything at all is a damned miracle. "Where?"

Miles is a head shorter than me and built lean, his skin covered in fine green scales. He's also telepathic. He shields his eyes and looks up to the crow's nest. A few moments later, he points. "There."

I follow his finger to see a figure in the water less than ten meters away. I tense, half raising the spear, before I register what I'm seeing. Pale skin. Long hair that's *hair* and not water weeds. A face that is decidedly more human than the merfolk I've come across in my years hunting with the Cŵn Annwn. "Not a mermaid."

Miles shrugs. "Then leave them. The sea will take care of it."

He always does this. If there's a change of plan, Miles would rather run it over than bend to adapt to new circumstances. There was a time when I was exactly the same way, cleaving to the rules without any allowance for nuance. It's certainly easier. Allowing the sea to take this person instead of bringing them onboard and triggering the decision between death and joining the crew would be less of a headache.

It's still not how we do things.

I have enough blood on my hands to last lifetimes. I try to avoid adding more whenever possible. I pass over the spear. "Might be a local."

"No local is going to be out *here*." He shakes his head, the move too sharp to be strictly human. "We haven't seen another ship in days, and there's been no storms to sweep one down, let alone to bring a survivor into our path. They're a trespasser."

Probably. Likely even.

That doesn't mean I'm going to let the sea take them without checking, and then offering them their choice. The whole purpose of the Cŵn Annwn is to protect Threshold and all the realms connected to it by portals on the islands scattered across the vast sea. Not all the islands contain portals, though, and there *are* citizens of the realm who are supposed to fall under our protection as well.

Not that everyone remembers that. At least not when it doesn't suit them.

I wait for The Crimson Hag to get a little closer to the person. I could dive in and retrieve them, but there's no reason to go through those theatrics. Instead, I focus my power and extend it, scooping the person out of the water and bringing them carefully over to the deck.

The crew eyes these goings on with some interest. It's not every day we haul people out of the sea, and it's even rarer that they're still alive when we do.

I crouch next to our catch and take a better look at them. A woman, human or from one of the realms where they're more humanoid than not. She's wearing clothing that looks unfamiliar, a bag strapped to her back, so it takes me a moment to place the denim pants. Jeans. That narrows down the options of her origin considerably. They cling to a body that's lush, thick thighs, broad hips, soft stomach. Her black shirt clings to her torso, hinting at small breasts.

I jerk my gaze up to her face, determined not to stand here ogling an unconscious woman, but there's no relief to be found. She has round cheeks, a full mouth, and wide-set eyes. Her skin is pale enough that I want to get her under cover before the sun has its way with her, and her hair color is hard to determine while wet, but I think is a few shades lighter than my own.

A spear flashes into view. I throw out my hand to stop it, but I'm too slow. "Fuck!" I tense, but it hovers in the air, it's point a mere inch from her chest. A flare of violet magic surges and then disappears and the spear clatters to the deck.

I spin on Miles. "What the fuck are you doing?"

"My job," he says flatly. "She's not one of ours."

No, she certainly isn't. I don't recognize the magic, but based on her human looks, I'd wager she's a witch. No reason for that to intrigue me. It just means she'd be an asset if we turn her. "Our *job* is to offer a choice."

"The Cŵn Annwn has no use for women like her."

I open my mouth to tell him where he can fuck right off to, but her eyes fly open, stalling me. She takes us in with a single look and then slams her hand to her chest. Magic rises in a wave that pushes me back a full meter before I get my magic up in a shield. Several of my people aren't so lucky. Splashes sound, quickly followed by the call, "Man overboard!"

Miles goes for the spear, but she kicks it away before he can get his hands on it. "Where the hell am I?" Her voice is hoarse, as if she was in the sea longer than I realized.

"You, don't move." I point at her and then turn my glare on Miles. "Get those people out of the water. Now."

For a moment, I think he might argue, but he finally gives a sharp nod and starts snapping commands to the crew. Within a few minutes, we've fished out the fallen crew and ensured there was no permanent damage done to the ship itself.

While I've been dealing with this, the woman has done some looking of her own. She surveys my ship in a way that makes my skin tight, like she's assessing every inch visible for value. I know what that look means.

Thief.

Sure enough, she has something in her hand that she's fiddling with. I recognize it instantly, and my hand goes to my hip where my flask usually is. Gone now, taken by her quick hands while I assumed the was unconscious.

Maybe Miles is right about her.

I shake my head sharply. A choice. We always offer a choice. It's the very essence of what separates us from the monsters we hunt. *Their* victims are not offered anything resembling mercy.

She catches me watching her play with the flask and grins, completely unrepentant. "Should I call you Captain?" Her voice is throaty, and she sinks enough innuendo into the question to sink the Hag.

I take a step toward her before I catch myself. This woman is no siren—they're all but extinct—but she has a pull all her own. "You're aboard The Crimson Hag, a vessel of the Cŵn Annwn."

Interest sharpens her eyes. I belatedly realize they're a green that makes me think of magic and lush forests. She leans closer and makes a show of looking me up and down. "Funny, but you don't look like a hound."

"A hound," I repeat.

"Mmm." Her gaze snags on my chest and stays there. "Hounds of Annwn and all that. I know my Welsh myths."

I have nothing to say to that. We aren't a myth. We never were. But history has a way of becoming myth if given enough time and distance. There are stories about the Cŵn Annwn in a lot of realms. As long as there's been Threshold acting as its given name between the realms, there have been the Cŵn Annwn, protecting it. If the original group occasionally shifted forms and hunted in other realms...

Well, we try not to draw attention from the originals for a reason.

Which means not breaking the laws. They exist for a reason. "You have a choice. Join the Cŵn Annwn or be given back to the sea."

"Wow, that's an interesting choice, very original and not at all overdone." She rolls her eyes.

It strikes me that she's not at all afraid of me. I blink. I don't know what to do with that. Even the people in Threshold, the ones it is our entire purpose to protect, fear us. I have a reputation I've worked hard for, and while I've never hurt a local, they know what else I've done. They can't help but know it, and fear me. They *should* fear me. It's safer that way. "It's the only choice you have," I snap.

"Cute." She turns and looks around once more before facing me again. "But I'm abstaining for making any choices. The lizard man tried to stab me in the heart before he knew I was awake, so forgive me if I don't want to join your little murder club."

"But you'll steal from us." I hold out a hand. "Give it back."

"Oh, this little thing?" She holds up the flask as if she's never seen it before. "It's mine. Old family heirloom."

"Why you—" I bring myself up before I reach for her. "What's your name?" I demand.

"Evelyn." She flips the flask up and catches it deftly. "There's one all-encompassing rule of the universe, dear Captain. I'm surprised you don't know it."

Even as I know I'll regret asking, I sigh. "What's the rule?"

"Finder's keepers." She grins. "This is mine. I won't give it back, no matter how much you snap and snarl at me. Really, you're taking the hound thing too literally. It's embarrassing."

That's about enough of that. She's obviously going to be difficult, and while that shouldn't be a death sentence, I can't let her undermine me in front of my crew. Like all ships of the Cŵn Annwn, we elect our captains by a vote. My authority only exists as long as my crew has faith in me, and nothing will make them lose it faster than this little witch mouthing off, not a lick of fear on her face.

If I lose the captaincy, Miles will take the vote. The first thing he'll do is stab that spear right through her heart.

I draw my power to me, as easy as breathing, and wrap her up in it. Evelyn squeaks, but I gag her before she can keep running her mouth, sealing her jaw shut. Her eyes go wide and then narrow, promising retribution.

I lift her easily off the deck and toss her over my shoulder. Several of the crewman laugh when she makes an indignant noise, but Miles watches with narrowed eyes.

Let him watch.

She's not taking this seriously, but people often don't when they mistakenly go through a portal and end up somewhere they're not supposed to be. Not until it's too late. The laws are the laws, but that doesn't mean I can't bend them a bit.

Not even for a cute, mouthy little witch.

FIND HUNT on Dark Waters here!